A PASSIONATE
REUNION IN FIJI

A PASSIONATE REUNION IN FIJI

MICHELLE SMART

MILLS & BOON

First published in Great Britain 2019
by Mills & Boon, an imprint of HarperCollins*Publishers*
1 London Bridge Street, London, SE1 9GF

Large Print edition 2020

© 2019 Michelle Smart

ISBN: 978-0-263-08413-9

MIX
Paper from
responsible sources
FSC
www.fsc.org   FSC C007454

This book is produced from independently certified
FSC™ paper to ensure responsible forest management. For
more information visit www.harpercollins.co.uk/green.

Printed and bound in Great Britain
by CPI Group (UK) Ltd, Croydon, CR0 4YY

This is for Keanu Reeves,
my teenage object of lust,
who, like a fine wine,
grows only better with age.

CHAPTER ONE

LIVIA BRIATORE CLIMBED the metal steps to the sleek jet's cabin, her heart hammering so hard she felt the vibrations in the tips of her hair. The sun was setting, the growing darkness perfectly matching the darkness that had enveloped her these recent months.

The flight crew, the same crew from when she'd first boarded this plane over two years ago, greeted her warmly but with questions ringing from their eyes.

Livia responded with a smile but the effort was such the muscles of her mouth protested. She didn't think she'd smiled once these past four months.

Sick dread swirled in her stomach. Clamping her teeth together, she straightened her spine and raised her chin, then stepped into the luxurious cabin where she was destined to spend the next twenty-six hours flying to Fiji.

Immediately her senses were assailed by the familiar smell of expensive upholstery mingled with the musky yet citrusy scent of the man on the plush leather seat, a laptop open before him.

She almost doubled over with the strength of the pain that punched through her stomach.

The first time Livia had stepped on this plane her heart had pounded with excitement and anticipation. Her body had run amok with brand-new feelings.

That first time in this plane, taking off from this very same airport in Rome, she had been filled with more happiness than she had known existed. The man whose attention was currently fixed on his laptop had hardly been able to wait for take-off before dragging her into the bedroom to make love to her.

All that was left of the flame of the passion that had seen them married within a month of meeting was ashes.

She blinked the painful memories away and forced her leaden legs forward.

She'd made a promise and she would keep it, however much it hurt.

The plane had four luxury window seats facing each other with the aisle between them. Massimo had raised his partition and when she took the seat diagonal to his, all she could see of him were his shoes. They were as buffed and polished as they always had been, a quirk she had thought adorable. Her husband was the least vain man she had ever met but he always took pride in his footwear.

She fastened her seat belt then laced her fingers tightly together to stop herself giving in to the need to bite her nails. She'd had an expensive gel treatment done on them the day before, masking that they were all bitten to the quick. She didn't want Massimo to see them like that. She couldn't bear for him to look at her and see the signs of her broken heart.

Livia had patched her heart back up. She'd licked her wounds and stitched herself back together. That was the only good thing about her childhood. It had taught her how to survive.

She would survive the next four days too.

Four days and then she need never see him again.

The captain's voice came over the tannoy system, informing them they were cleared to take off. His words brought Massimo to life. The partition acting as a barrier came down as he closed his laptop and stored it away, then fastened his seat belt. Not once did he look at her but Livia was aware of every movement he made. Her heart bloomed to see the muscles of his tall, lean body flex beneath the expensive navy shirt with the sleeves carelessly rolled up, the buttons around his strong neck undone. No doubt he'd ripped the tie he would have worn to the conference from his neck the moment he'd left the venue. A maverick even by usual standards, Massimo conformed to rules only when *he* judged it necessary. She supposed the engineering conference in London he'd been guest of honour at had been an occasion he'd decided was worthy of bothering with an actual suit.

Livia only knew he'd been in London because his PA had casually mentioned it in her email when they'd been making the arrangements for today.

It wasn't until the plane taxied down the runway that the soulful caramel eyes she had once stared into with wonder finally met her gaze. It was the briefest of glances before he turned his attention to the window beside his head but it was enough for Livia's stomach to flip over and her throat to tighten.

Massimo's face was one she'd been familiar with long before they'd met. Employed as his grandfather's private nurse, she'd stared at the large Briatore family portrait that had hung in his grandfather's living room too many times to count. Her gaze had always been drawn to the only member whose smile appeared forced. It was a beautiful face. Slightly long with high cheekbones, a strong Roman nose and a wide firm mouth, it was a chameleon of a face, fitting for a construction worker, a banker or a poet. That it belonged to one of the richest self-made billionaires in the world was irrelevant. She would have been drawn to that face no matter who he was.

Seeing him in the flesh for the first time, in

the church his sister was getting married in, had been like having all the oxygen sucked out of her.

The first time she'd seen him smile for real her insides had melted as if she'd been injected with liquid sunshine. *She* had brought that smile out in him. She couldn't even remember what she'd said, only that after hours of sidelong glances at each other throughout the wedding ceremony and the official photographs, she'd gone to the bar of the hotel the reception was being held in and suddenly the air around her had become electrified. She'd known before even turning her head that he'd come to stand beside her. Her tongue, usually so razor sharp, had tied itself in knots. Whatever she'd said in those first awkward moments had evoked that smile and in that instant all the awkwardness disappeared and it was as if they had known each other for ever.

And now he couldn't even bring himself to look at her.

She had no idea how they were going to get through a weekend with his family, celebrating his grandfather's ninetieth birthday, pretending to still be together.

Massimo watched an illuminated Rome disappear beneath the clouds and tried to clear the hot cloud that was the mess in his head.

When he'd agreed to speak at the engineering conference in London, it had made sense to fly to Rome afterwards and collect Livia en route. It had been logical.

He'd assumed that after four months apart, being with her again would be no big deal. He hadn't missed her in the slightest. Not that there had been time to miss her with all the hours he'd been putting in. Without the burden of a hot-tempered wife demanding his attention, he'd been able to devote himself to his multiple businesses just as he had before she'd collided into his life and torn it inside out. The day she'd left, he'd bought himself the bed for his office which the mere suggestion of had so angered her. He'd slept in it most nights since. It was far more comfortable than the blanket on the sofa he'd used the nights he'd worked late and decided it wasn't worth driving home.

He hadn't anticipated that his blood would become hot and sticky and his hands clammy just to land in his home city and be under the same sky as her again.

And now that she was here, in the cabin of his plane, every cell in his body, dormant all this time apart, had awoken.

He could curse his logical mind. Why hadn't he insisted she fly to Los Angeles, where he was scheduled to refuel, and board his plane there? He couldn't have her fly all the way to Fiji separately from him—that would defeat the whole purpose of her being there—but he could have engineered things so they only had to spend a minimal amount of time on his plane together, not the full twenty-six hours it would take to travel to the other side of the world.

For the return journey he would fly with her to Australia and charter a plane to fly her back to Italy.

He'd listed all the excuses he could have made to avoid bringing her with him but it had all boiled down to one thing. This was for his grandfather, Jimmy Seibua. His terminally ill grandfather, who'd taken a cruise from Rome to Fiji with his family and an army of medical personnel in attendance and had arrived on the island three days ago. This weekend was all that had been keeping his grandfather alive, this one last visit to the homeland he'd left as a twenty-two-year-old the spark giving him the fight needed to beat the odds. Jimmy would celebrate his ninetieth birthday on the Fijian island of his birth, now owned by Massimo, with the family he loved. His grandfather thought of Livia as part of his family. He loved her as a granddaughter. His only regret at Massimo marrying her was that it meant he lost the private nurse who had tended to him with such care during his first battle with cancer.

And, whatever his own feelings towards his estranged wife, Massimo knew Livia loved Jimmy too.

'Are you going to spend the entire flight ignoring me?'

Massimo clenched his jaw as Livia's direct husky tones penetrated his senses, speaking their native Italian.

That was the thing with his wife. She was always direct. If she wasn't happy about something she made damned sure you knew about it. For a long time the object of her unhappiness had been Massimo. Her declaration that she was leaving him had come as no surprise, only relief. Marriage to Livia had gone from being passionate and invigorating to being like a war zone. And she wondered why he'd spent so much time at work? The nights they had spent together those last few months had been with her cold back firmly turned to him. She'd even started wearing nightshirts.

He swallowed back the lump that had suddenly appeared in his throat and finally allowed his gaze to fall on her properly.

The lump he'd tried to shift grew but he opened his mouth and dragged the words through it. 'You've had your hair cut.'

Her beautiful thick, dark chestnut hair, which had fallen like a sheet down to her lower back, now fell in layers to rest on her shoulders in loose curls. It was lighter too, streaks of honey blonde carefully blending with her natural colour. Livia was not the most beautiful woman in the world but to his eyes she was stunning. It was the whole package. A sexy firecracker with a dirty laugh. He'd heard that laugh echo through the walls of the church while they'd waited for his sister, the bride, to arrive and when he'd spotted the woman behind it he'd felt the fabric of his existence shift. He'd grabbed the first available opportunity to speak to her and had been blown away to discover she had a thirsty, inquisitive mind. He'd been smitten. In Livia he'd found the woman he'd never known he'd been searching for. Or so he'd thought.

Her dark brown eyes, always so expressive, widened before a choked laugh flew from her mouth. 'That's all you can think to say?'

She didn't wait for a response; unbuckling her seat belt and springing to her feet.

She'd lost weight, he noted hazily.

Her kissable plump lips were tight as she stalked past him, the bathroom door closing sharply a moment later.

Massimo rubbed his jaw and struggled to get air into his closed lungs.

He hadn't expected this to be easy but it was a thousand times harder than he'd envisaged.

Livia sat on the closed toilet seat and hugged her arms across her chest, willing the threatening tears back. She hadn't expected this tumult of emotions to engulf her or for the ache in her chest to hurt so much.

She had shed enough tears for this man, so many she'd thought herself all cried out.

Massimo had never loved her. That was the truth she needed to keep reminding herself of.

But she had loved him. Truly, madly, deeply.

And in return he'd broken her.

The worst of it was he had no idea. For all his high intelligence, her husband had the emotional depth of an earthworm. She'd just been too blind to see it.

She closed her eyes and took three long inhalations.

There was no point in driving herself crazy with her thoughts. She had loved him once and while echoes of that love still beat in her heart they weren't real. She didn't love him any more. She was only there to honour the promise she'd made to him the day he'd let her go without a solitary word of fight to make her stay.

He'd wanted her gone. He'd been relieved. She'd seen it in his eyes.

Three more deep breaths and she got back to her feet and flushed the unused toilet.

She was Livia Briatore, formerly Livia Esposito, daughter of Pietro Esposito, Don Fortunato's most trusted clan member and henchman until her father's gangland murder when she'd been only eight. She'd been raised in the Secondigliano surrounded by drugs and brutal violence and she'd learned from an early age to show no fear. To show nothing.

Escaping Naples to study nursing in Rome had been like learning to breathe. Dropping her guard had not been easy—constantly checking over her shoulder when she walked a street was a habit it had taken many years to break—but she had forged a new life for herself and the joy it had given her had been worth the anxiety that had gnawed at her to be separated from her siblings. Life had gone from being a constant knot in her belly to being an adventure. She'd learned to laugh. With Massimo she had learned to love.

But her old protective barrier had never fully gone. It had sat patiently inside her waiting to be slipped back on.

To get through the next four days she needed that barrier. She needed to keep her guard up, not as protection against Massimo but as protection against her own foolish heart.

She took her seat and was not surprised to find Massimo working again on his laptop.

This time he raised his eyes from the screen to look at her. 'I've ordered us coffee. Did you want anything to eat?'

'I've eaten,' she answered with strained politeness, not adding that all she'd eaten that day had been half a slice of toast. Her stomach had been too tight and cramped to manage anything else. The countdown to seeing Massimo again had wrecked the little equilibrium she'd regained for herself.

It was hardly surprising that there was an awkwardness between them but they had a long flight ahead and she didn't want to spend it in uncomfortable silence. 'How have you been?'

He pulled a face and turned his attention back to his laptop. 'Busy.'

She dug her fake nails into her thighs. How she hated that word. It was the word he'd always used to justify never being there. 'Are you too busy to stop working for five minutes and talk?'

'I have data to interpret and an analysis to send.'

Two years ago he would have explained both the data and analysis to her, assuming rightly that she would find it interesting. The truth was she had found everything about Massimo interesting. Enthralling. The workings of his brain had never failed to astonish her. How could they not? This was the man who'd used his downtime from his computer engineering degree to create a web-based platform game that had taken the world by storm and which he'd sold upon his graduation for two hundred million US dollars. That money had been the linchpin for his move to America, where he'd formed his company, Briatore Technologies, whilst simultaneously studying for a PhD in energy physics, followed by a second PhD in applied physics and material sciences. His company, of which he was still the sole owner, now employed thousands worldwide, creating environmentally friendly solutions for many of the world's greatest carbon-related threats. He was on a one-man mission to save the planet one invention at a time. That he'd earned himself a fortune in the process was almost incidental. Only a month ago he'd been named in the top thirty of the world's most powerful people and in the top fifty of the world's richest.

It would have been so easy for him to make her feel stupid but he never had. Anything she didn't understand—which when it came to his work was most things—he would explain patiently but never patronisingly, his face lighting up when she grasped the finer details of something, like how a lithium ion battery worked and what carbon capture meant on a practical level.

She had been so thrilled that this man, clever, rich, successful and with a face and body to make the gods envious, had been as seemingly enthralled with her as she had been with him that she'd been blind to his emotional failings. Once the first flush of lust had worn off he'd retreated into the all-consuming world he'd created for himself, hiding himself away from the woman he'd married.

She wished she knew what she'd done to make him back away from her but every time she'd tried to get him to open up, the further into his shell he'd retreated.

The silence, filled intermittently by the sounds of Massimo tapping on the laptop's keyboard, grew more oppressive.

She watched him work. The familiar furrow of concentration was etched on his brow. How could he tune her out so effectively?

But as she watched him she noticed subtle changes. Flecks of white around the temples of his thick black hair that had never been there before. The full beard, as if he'd given up the bother of shaving altogether. Dark rings around his eyes as if he'd given up sleep along with shaving. Not that he had ever slept much. His brain was too busy for sleep.

Livia swallowed back the pang that had crept through her. Massimo was thirty-six years old; old enough to not look after himself if that was what he wanted.

He reached absently for the strong black coffee on the desk beside his laptop and took a large sip. His attention did not stray from the screen before him. He tapped something else onto the keyboard. The sound was akin to nails being dragged down a chalkboard.

Suddenly she could bear it no more. Jumping back to her feet, she took the three steps to him and slammed his laptop lid down.

CHAPTER TWO

MASSIMO CLENCHED HIS teeth together and placed a protective hand on his laptop to prevent Livia from snatching hold of it and throwing it onto the floor. 'What was that for?'

Diminutive though she was in height, in presence she was larger than life and right then, standing over him, she seemed magnified, the anger rippling from her in waves. 'We've been in the air for an hour and you've spared me only ten words.'

'Twenty-six,' he corrected through gritted teeth. 'I have spoken twenty-six words.'

'And now you're being pedantic as well as rude.' She pulled her hair together in a fist then released it. 'How are we supposed to convince your grandfather and the rest of your family that we're still together if you won't look at me or talk to me?'

'I'm not being rude. This is a very important time for me. On Monday we are running the prototypes on…'

'I don't *care*,' she interrupted with a cry. 'Whatever you're working on, I do not care. I'm here as a favour to you for your grandfather's benefit. The least you can do is treat me with some respect.'

'If I'm being disrespectful then I apologise,' he answered stiffly, biting back the retort of *what did you expect?* Livia had been the one to walk out on their marriage, not him. She had been the one to laugh in his face when he suggested they have a child. How did she expect him to be around her?

Damned if *he* knew how to act around her. Focusing his attention on the screen before him was the only tool he had to drive out the tumultuous emotions ripping through him. That these emotions were still there defied belief but Livia had always been able to induce feelings in him that had no place in his world, feelings that went far deeper than mere lust and friendship. She took up too much head space. She distracted him. That would have been easy to deal with if she'd only distracted his head when he'd been at home.

'I don't want your apologies. You don't mean it. You never do. Your apologies are meaningless.'

It was an accusation she had thrown at him many times and usually preceded an escalation of her temper, which only got wilder when he refused to engage. Massimo disliked meaningless confrontation, considered it a waste of energy, and would walk away when she refused to listen to reason.

Unfortunately, right now there was nowhere for him to walk away to. To escape to.

Keeping his own temper in check—keeping a cool head when all those around him lost theirs was something he took pride in— Massimo inhaled slowly through his nose and gazed at the angry face before him. 'What I'm working on is important. I'll be finished before we land in Los Angeles. We can spend the time between Los Angeles and Fiji talking if that's what you want.'

She laughed without any humour then flopped onto the seat opposite his and glared at him. 'Great. You're going to do me the huge favour of talking to me if *I* want. Thank you. You're too kind.'

She'd folded her arms across her chest, slightly raising her breasts. He knew she hadn't done it deliberately—intimacy between them had died long before she'd called time on their marriage itself—but it distracted him enough for a sliver of awareness to pierce his armoury.

Livia had a body that could make a man weep. Even dressed as she was now, fully covered in tight faded jeans and a roll-neck black jumper, her feminine curves were undeniable. The first time he'd made love to her he'd thought he'd died and gone to heaven. Her virginity had surprised and delighted him. Surprised him because he would never have believed a twenty-four-year-old woman with such a dirty laugh and who carried herself with such confidence could be a virgin. Delighted him because it had marked her as his in a primal way he'd never experienced before.

Sex had never been a great need for him. When he'd shot up from a scrawny teenager into the frame he now inhabited, he'd suddenly found women throwing themselves at him, something that had only increased when he'd sold his web-based game after graduation and become worth a fortune. If he'd been in the mood he'd been happy to oblige, finding sex a satiating yet fleeting diversion from his work. Livia was the first woman he'd been truly intimate with. When they had first got together they'd been unable to keep their hands off each other. For the first time in his life Massimo had found himself consumed by lust.

The loss of that intimacy had not been his choice. Their marriage had disintegrated to such an extent that the nights he had made it home, they'd slept back to back. A man could take only so much rejection from his own wife before he stopped bothering.

Had she taken a lover? It was a thought that sent a stabbing motion plunging into his chest and for a moment he closed his eyes and breathed the pain away.

It was none of his business if she'd taken a lover and it would be unreasonable to expect her to have remained celibate during their separation. If not for his grandfather they would already be divorced.

'When did you last see your grandfather?' she asked suddenly, cutting through his attempts to concentrate on the screen in front of him rather than the bombshell opposite.

Livia felt only fleeting satisfaction to see the caramel eyes raise to meet hers.

'Why do you ask?'

'Because when I saw him the day before he set sail for Fiji he complained that you hadn't been in touch. I emailed Lindy about it.'

Lindy was Massimo's PA, a dragon of a woman who ran his business life. She was the only person in the world who knew their marriage was over in all but name. As far as their respective families were concerned, they were still together.

When they'd married, Livia had hoped Massimo's new status would encourage him to see more of his family but it hadn't worked that way. In their two years of shared life they had spent one Christmas with his family and that had been it. Livia had made numerous visits from their house in Los Angeles to Italy alone, visiting her youngest brother and dropping in on Massimo's family, all of whom she adored.

Since they'd gone their separate ways, her frequent visits had continued. They were used to her visiting alone so Massimo's absence had gone unremarked. Only Madeline, Massimo's sister, had the perception to see that anything was wrong but as she had a newborn child to take care of, her perception skills were less honed than usual. The ache that formed in Livia's heart as she held Madeline's baby only added to the ache already there but she would have been helpless to resist cradling the tiny bundle in her arms even if she didn't have a show to perform.

None of the Briatores or Espositos had any idea she was back on Italian soil permanently. Whenever she was asked about Massimo— who rarely bothered to message his family and had never met his niece—she would say he was busy with work, satisfied that she wasn't telling a lie. Massimo was *always* busy with work. Always. She'd lived with his grandfather as his private nurse for nine months and in that time Massimo hadn't made one trip home.

She'd accepted the family line that Massimo was too busy to fly home from California regularly but had come to her own private conclusion during their marriage that it was nothing to do with his schedule preventing him from spending more time with his family. He simply didn't want to.

She would be glad when these evasions of the truth could be done with and they could tell his family they had separated. She hated lying, even if only by omission.

'Lindy mentioned it,' he admitted stiffly.

'Did you do anything about it?'

'I called him on the ship. He sounded fine.' His gaze dropped back to his laptop.

'He isn't fine.' Livia's heart had broken to see how frail Jimmy had become. The elderly yet vital man who'd waged such a strong battle against his first diagnosis of cancer was fading, too weak to fly both legs of the mammoth journey to Fiji. It had been decided that a cruise was the safest way to get him to the other side of the world. Jimmy wanted to spend his ninetieth birthday with all his family around him, see corners of the world he'd never visited before and tread the soil he'd been raised on one last time.

Everything for him was now one last time.

'I know that.'

'Will you spend some proper time with him this weekend?' she asked. It was pointless adding that spending real time with Massimo was Jimmy's greatest wish. It was his parents' greatest wish too.

Massimo thought the gift of his money was enough. When he'd made his fortune, he'd bought his entire family new homes of their own and a car each. As his wealth had increased so had his generous gifts to them. It had been Massimo who'd paid for the private treatment during Jimmy's first diagnosis and all the associated costs including the agency fees for Livia's wages as his live-in nurse. It was Massimo who had bought the island his grandfather came from and spent a fortune building a complex for the entire family to stay on. It was Massimo footing the bill for the cruise the rest of the family were taking with Jimmy to reach the island. He'd chartered an ocean liner for their sole use.

Yet for all his generosity, he was spectacularly blind to the fact his family would much rather have his presence than his presents. He also seemed blind to the fact that time was running out for his grandfather.

'Yes.'

'You'll leave your laptop and phone switched off?'

'You know I can't do that.'

'I know you *won't* do that.'

His jaw clenched. 'We can talk about this later.'

She laughed mockingly. 'Later. Of course. Everything is always *later* with you, isn't it?'

Without any warning, Massimo slammed his fist against the panel beside his seat. 'And everything still has to be *now* with you. I said we could talk once I have completed my work but, as always, you don't listen. This is important and needs my attention. If you can't wait patiently for me to finish then I suggest you take yourself to the bedroom and give your mouth a rest.'

Massimo refused to feel guilt for his outburst, even when Livia's face paled before him.

True to form, she refused to let him get the last word, getting to her feet slowly and glowering at him. 'If anyone has a problem with listening it's you. If it doesn't involve your precious work then it's insignificant to you. It's been four months since you last saw me and you haven't even cared to ask how I've been. If I'd had any doubts that leaving you was the best thing I could do, an hour in your company has proven me right. You never cared for me. You've never cared for anyone.'

She walked away, not to the bedroom but to her original seat. There was dignity in the way she moved that, despite the acrimony that thickened the air between them, touched him. Livia was a strange mix of toughness and vulnerability, traits that had first moved him then infuriated him. Her toughness meant she did not know how to back down from an argument but the underlying vulnerability found her easily wounded. He'd never known the words to say to repair the wounds he'd unwittingly inflicted on her. Eventually he'd stopped trying.

Her partition rose and she disappeared from sight.

Massimo sighed his relief and rubbed his eyes. He hadn't slept in over twenty-four hours and was exhausted.

Ringing the bell, he ordered a fresh coffee when the stewardess appeared. Caffeine and sugar would keep him awake long enough to get his analysis done. Maybe then he'd be able to catch some sleep.

He tuned out Livia's husky voice when the stewardess turned her attention to his wife.

But he couldn't tune out her presence.

The data on the screen before him blurred. His head felt so heavy. All of him felt heavy, a weight compressing him from the top down and, even with the importance of the work that needed to be done, he found his thoughts drifting to the early days of their marriage, days when he'd believed nothing could come between them.

Nothing *had* come between them. Only themselves.

Livia tried to concentrate on the movie she'd selected from the thousands stored on the in-flight entertainment system—a system Massimo had had installed for her benefit—but the storyline passed her by in a haze. The first movie, a comedy, had passed her by too. This second one was a critically acclaimed thriller guaranteed to keep her tear ducts intact but, even with the sound on her headphones turned up high to drown out the incessant tapping of Massimo's fingers on his keyboard, he was all she could think about.

How had it come to this? How could a marriage formed with such passion and joy disintegrate into such bitterness?

Movement caught her attention and she removed her headphones and straightened as the head stewardess approached to see if she would like anything.

'A blanket would be nice, thanks,' she replied. The air-conditioning on Massimo's jet was always set to freezing.

The blanket delivered, Livia was suddenly struck by the cabin's silence.

Lowering her partition, she looked across at Massimo.

He'd fallen asleep.

His laptop was still open but the man himself was fast asleep, upright in his seat, his mouth slightly open as he breathed in and out heavily.

A tightness formed in her chest as she watched until, without thinking, she got to her feet and padded over to him.

For a long time, hardly daring to breathe, she drank in the features of the man she had once loved so much. His Fijian ancestry was stronger in him than in his sister. His skin was a deep olive, his thick hair the most beautiful shade of ebony. She'd liked it when he forgot to cut it, and had spent many happy hours snuggled on the sofa with him, Massimo talking, his head on her lap, Livia content to simply listen to his wonderful rich, deep voice and run her fingers through his hair. It was the closest to peace she had ever felt in her life.

She'd tried so hard to hold onto what they had but he had slipped away from her with the same ease her fingers had run through his hair.

Her throat closed, Livia carefully draped the blanket she'd been about to use for herself on his lap. She wanted to press the button that would tilt the chair back and turn it into a bed but was afraid the motion would wake him. Struck again by the dark circles around his eyes, she wondered when he'd last had a decent night's sleep. Or the last time he'd had a decent meal.

The compulsion to reach out her hand and stroke her fingers over his high cheekbones, to feel the texture of his skin on hers, to run her fingers through his hair…it all hit her so fast that her hand was inches from his face before she realised what she was about to do and stopped herself.

Her heart thumped wildly and for a moment she couldn't breathe.

Putting her hand to her chest, she backed away, afraid to be this close to him.

Afraid of what it did to her.

Massimo's eyes opened with a start.

He blinked rapidly, disorientated.

His laptop was still open but had put itself into sleep mode.

Had *he* fallen asleep?

Getting to his feet to stretch his legs, he felt a sudden chill on his thighs and gazed down in astonishment at the blanket that had fallen to the floor.

Where had that come from?

He stared over at Livia. Her partition was still up but, standing, he could see her clearly. She'd reclined her chair and was watching something on the television with her headphones in. A blanket covered her whole body up to her chin.

'Did you put a blanket on me?' He didn't mean to sound so accusatory but the thought of her doing that…

Her face turned towards him and she pulled the headphones off. 'Did you say something?'

Before he could answer one of the cabin crew entered. 'We will be landing in twenty minutes.'

The moment they were alone again, Massimo turned back to Livia. 'How long was I asleep?'

She shrugged.

He swore under his breath. He hadn't finished his analysis. Damn it, he'd promised the project manager that he would have it in his inbox before he reached the office that morning.

He bit back the demand he wanted to throw at her as to why she hadn't woken him and sat back down.

Livia had put the blanket on him. He knew that with a deep certainty and he didn't know if it was that simple gesture or that he was now behind on where he needed to be work-wise that made his guts feel as if acid had been poured in them.

He felt close to snapping. Virulent emotions were coursing through him and his wife, the cause of all his angst, was reclined in her seat as nonchalant as could be.

But knowing her as well as he did, he knew her nonchalance was a sham. Livia did not do nonchalance.

Why had she put a blanket on him?

His eyes were better able to focus after his short sleep but, with their landing imminent, he put his laptop away and folded his desk up and secured it, all the while hating that he was fully aware of Livia sorting her own seating area out, avoiding looking at him as much as he avoided looking at her.

Los Angeles couldn't come soon enough.

Not another word was exchanged until the plane had landed safely.

Needing to escape the strange febrile atmosphere that seemed to have infected his flight crew as much as them, Massimo grabbed his laptop and got to his feet but the moment he left his seat, Livia was there facing him in the aisle, holding her bag tightly, clearly ready to make her own escape.

He stepped to one side to let her pass but she stepped to the same side too.

Their eyes met. Their gaze held, only momentarily, but long enough for him to see the pain she had become a master at hiding from him.

A sharp compression lanced his chest, as if his heart had become a rose in full bloom, its thorns spearing into him.

And then she blinked, cast her gaze to the

floor, murmured, 'Excuse me,' and brushed past him.

Massimo swallowed away the lump in his throat and left his plane by the other exit.

CHAPTER THREE

TWO HOURS AFTER landing in Los Angeles, they were cleared to take off for the second leg of their mammoth journey to Fiji.

Livia had returned to the plane before Massimo. She guessed he'd gone to the private executive lounge in the airport to work. She'd taken herself for a walk, keeping her phone in her hand for the alert that the plane had refuelled and she could get back on, and tried to get hold of Gianluca, her youngest sibling. He hadn't answered and hadn't called her back either. She'd had no wish to go sightseeing or do any of the things most visitors with a short layover at LAX would do. Just breathing the air brought back the awful feelings that had lived in her the last dying months of their marriage.

She hated Los Angeles. She hated California. She'd loathed living there. For a place known as the Golden State, her life there had been devoid of sunshine.

At first, she'd enjoyed the novelty of it all. Compared to Naples and Rome it was huge. Everything was so much bigger. Even the sky and the sun that shone in it appeared greater and brighter. But then loneliness had seeped its way in. She had no friends there and no means to make them. Unlike Massimo, who spoke fluent English, her own English was barely passable. The glass home they'd shared was forty kilometres from downtown LA. An intensely private man, Massimo had deliberately chosen a home far from prying eyes. There were no neighbours. The household staff spoke only English and Spanish.

She'd become sick with longing for home.

Massimo hadn't understood. He hadn't even tried.

But there hadn't been any sunshine since she'd left him and returned to her home in Italy either.

It was strange to experience taking off in her second sunset of the day. She should have slept during the first leg of the journey but sleep had been the last thing on her mind, the last thing she'd been capable of. The sun putting itself to sleep now in LA would soon be awakening in Rome.

She yawned and cast her eyes in Massimo's direction. His partition was raised again but she could still hear the tapping of his fingers on the keypad. So much for talking. Silence for them truly had become golden.

A member of the cabin crew brought her pillows and a duvet and turned her seat into a bed while Livia used the bathroom to change into pyjamas, remove her make-up and brush her teeth.

She thought of the plane's bedroom and its comfortable king-sized bed. An ache formed in the pit of her stomach to remember the glorious hours they had spent sharing it. Massimo would never begrudge her sleeping in it now but she couldn't do it. She couldn't sleep in a bed they had shared knowing that when she woke the pillow beside her would be unused. That had been hard enough to deal with when they'd been together.

Massimo was on his feet stretching his aching back when Livia returned to the cabin clutching her washbag. It was the same washbag she'd used when they'd been married and his heart tugged to see it.

She looked younger with her face free from make-up and plain cream pyjamas on. More vulnerable too.

The threads tugging at his heart tightened.

'I'm going to have a nightcap. Do you want one?'

Surprise lit her dark brown eyes before they fixed on his own freshly made-up bed. 'You're finished?'

He nodded. 'My apologies for it taking so long. I didn't factor in falling asleep.'

Her plump lips curved into the tiniest of smiles. 'I would have woken you but you looked exhausted.'

She looked exhausted. Her seat had been made up into a bed for her too but, however comfortable it was, it was not the same as sleeping in a proper bed. 'Why don't you sleep in our bed?'

Now the tiniest of winces flashed over her

face. 'I'll be fine here, thank you. You should use it—you only napped for a couple of hours.'

The only time he'd been in the jet's bedroom since she'd left him was to use the en-suite shower. Sleeping in the bed he'd shared with her...the thought alone had been enough to make his guts twist tightly.

To see the same reluctance reflected in her eyes twisted them even harder.

He removed a bottle of his favourite bourbon and two glasses from the bar as the stewardess came into the cabin with a bucket of ice. Massimo took it from her and arched an eyebrow in question at Livia.

She hesitated for a moment before nodding.

As the stewardess dimmed the lights and left the cabin, he poured them both a measure and handed a glass to Livia.

She took it with a murmured thanks, avoiding direct eye contact, carefully avoiding his touch. He could smell the mintiness of her toothpaste and caught a whiff of the delicately scented cream she used to remove her make-up and the moisturiser she finished her night-time routine with. The two combined into a scent that had always delighted his senses far more than her perfume, which in itself was beautiful. The perfume she sprayed herself with by day could be enjoyed by anyone who got close enough. Her night-time scent had always been for him alone.

Had any other man been lucky enough to smell it since they'd parted?

She sat on her bed and took a small sip of her bourbon. As she moved he couldn't help but notice the light sway of her naked breasts beneath the silk pyjama top.

Her nightwear was functional and obviously selected to cover every inch but the curves that had driven him to such madness were clearly delineated beneath the fabric and it took all his willpower to keep his gaze fixed on her face.

But her face had driven him to madness as much as the body had. With Livia it had always been the whole package. Everything about her. Madness.

After a few moments of stilted silence she said, 'Are you going to get some sleep too?'

Massimo knew what Livia was thinking: that having his own seat made into a bed was no indication that he actually intended to get any rest.

He shrugged and took a large sip of his bourbon, willing the smooth burn it made in his throat to flow through his veins and burn away the awareness searing his loins.

'If I can.' He raised his glass. 'This should help.' Enough of it would allow him a few precious hours of oblivion to the firecracker who would be sleeping at such close quarters to him.

'How long do we have until we reach Fiji?'

He checked his watch. 'Nine hours until we land at Nadi.'

'We get another flight from there?' Livia already knew the answer to this but the dimming of the lights seemed to have shrunk the generously proportioned cabin and given it an air of dangerous intimacy.

What was it about darkness that could change an atmosphere so acutely? Livia had grown up scared of the dark. The Secondigliano was a dangerous place in daylight. At night, all the monsters came out.

The dangers now were as different as night

and day compared to her childhood and adolescence but she felt them as keenly. With Massimo's face in shadows his handsome features took on a devilish quality that set her stomach loose with butterflies and her skin vibrating with awareness.

'I've chartered a Cessna to fly us to Seibua Island.'

'You managed to get the name changed?' She couldn't remember the original name of the island Massimo's grandfather had been born and raised on.

'The paperwork's still being sorted but I've been reliably informed it's been accepted.' He finished his drink and poured himself another, raising the bottle at her in an unspoken question.

She shook her head. Marriage to Massimo had given her a real appreciation of bourbon but too much alcohol had a tendency to loosen her tongue, which she was the first to admit didn't need loosening. It also loosened her inhibitions. She'd never had any inhibitions around Massimo before but to get through the weekend in one piece she needed them as greatly as she needed to keep her guard up around him. All of this would be easier to cope with if her heart didn't ache so much just to share the same air as him again.

'Are you going to buy a Cessna of your own to keep there?'

He grimaced and finally perched himself on his bed. The overhead light shone down on him. 'The yacht's already moored there and can be used as transport. Whether I buy a plane too depends on how often the family use the island.' The resort created on the island would be available for the entire extended family to use as and when they wished, free of charge. The only stipulation would be that they treated it with respect.

'Knowing your sister it will be often.' It was doubtful Massimo would ever use it. His idea of a holiday was to take a Sunday off work.

She caught the whisper of a smile on his firm mouth but it disappeared behind his glass as he took another drink.

'When did your family get there?'

'They arrived three days ago.'

'Have you been to the island yet?'

'I haven't had the time.'

She chewed her bottom lip rather than give voice to her thoughts that this was typical Massimo, never having the time for anything that didn't revolve around work. He'd jumped through hoops and paid an astronomical sum for the island but those hoops had been jumped through by his lawyers and accountants. He'd spent a further fortune having the complex for the family built but, again, he'd had little involvement past hiring the architects and transferring the cash. Livia had signed off on the initial blueprint for the complex in the weeks before she'd left him. She had no idea if he'd even bothered to do more than cast an eye over it.

There was no point in her saying anything. It would only be a rehash of a conversation they'd had many times before, a conversation that would only lead to an argument. Or, as usually happened, it would lead to her getting increasingly het up at his refusal to engage in the conversation and losing her temper, and Massimo walking away in contempt leaving her shouting at the walls.

In any case, Massimo's sidelining of anything that wasn't work-related was none of her business. Not any more. If he wanted to blow his own money on projects and assets he had no intention of enjoying then that was up to him. If he wanted to keep his family on the fringes of his life for eternity then that was up to him too. He wasn't an adolescent like her youngest brother, Gianluca, who'd been born seven months after their father's death.

There was hope for Gianluca. Unlike their other siblings, who had succumbed to life in the Secondigliano, Gianluca's humanity was still there. The question was whether he had the courage to take Livia's hand and join her far from the violence and drugs that were such an intrinsic part of the Espositos' lives before it was too late and he was sucked into a life of crime from which his only escape would be in a coffin.

It was too late for Pasquale, who like their dead father had risen high in Don Fortunato's ranks, and too late for Denise who had married one of Pasquale's equally ambitious friends and was currently pregnant with their second child. Livia's siblings and her mother all knew Livia's door was always open for them. Gianluca was the only one she allowed herself to hope for. He could still leave without repercussions just as she had but time was running out. He'd recently turned eighteen. Should Don Fortunato decide Gianluca was worthy of joining his guard he would strike soon.

The man Livia had married, a man who abhorred violence and anything to do with illegal drugs, had made his choice when he was only a few years older than Gianluca. He'd chosen to leave Italy and leave his family, just as his own grandfather had done seventy years before him. The difference was his grandfather had left Fiji for the love of his life, an Englishwoman, and set up home with her in England. When their daughter Sera had married an Italian, Jimmy and Elizabeth had moved again, this time to Italy so they could stay close to their daughter. For them, family came first above all else. They were as close as close could be. All except for Massimo himself.

He didn't want to change. He saw nothing

wrong with how he lived his life, nothing wrong with keeping a physical and emotional distance from the people who loved him. That was the choice he'd made and Livia had to respect that. She couldn't change it. She'd tried. When the realisation hit that his emotional distance from his family extended to her too, along with the recognition that this too would never change, she'd had no choice but to leave him.

She hadn't clawed her way out of the Secondigliano to spend her life as a trophy in a glass cabinet masquerading as a home.

While she had spent the past four months trying desperately to fix herself back together, for Massimo there had been nothing to fix. He'd got on with his life as if she'd never been a part of it.

Finishing her drink, she put the empty glass in the holder beside her bed and got under the covers. 'I'm going to get some sleep. Goodnight.' Then she turned her back on him and closed her eyes.

Massimo lay under his bed sheets, eyes wide open. He'd drunk enough bourbon to tranquillise an elephant but his mind was too busy. Except now it wasn't the project he'd spent over a year working on that stopped his mind switching off.

Turning his head, eyes adjusted to the dark, he watched the rhythmic rise and fall of Livia's duvet. He guessed she'd been asleep for around an hour now. He always knew when she was properly asleep and not just faking it. When she faked it, she lay rigid in absolute silence.

They'd slept together the first night they'd met—once they'd got talking at the hotel bar he hadn't let her out of his sight—and both of them had known it was no one-night stand. He'd been dozing in the aftermath, Livia wrapped in his arms, his body thrumming with the delights they'd just shared, when she'd mumbled something. That was his first experience of her sleep-talking. He'd quickly discovered that she talked a lot in her sleep. Sometimes the words were distinct. He remembered the feeling that had erupted through him the first time she'd mumbled his name. It had been ten times the magnitude of what he'd felt to be offered two hundred million dollars for the stupid game he'd developed during his boring university evenings.

But her dreams hadn't always been good. At least once a week he'd had to wake her from a bad one. The darkness of the life she'd lived until she'd left Naples at eighteen still haunted her.

Had another man woken her from the nightmares since she'd left him?

He pinched the bridge of his nose and willed the pain spearing him away.

Livia's sex life was no longer his business.

The thought of her with a lover was something that hadn't even occurred to him until she'd stepped onto his plane and now it was all he could think of.

In the four months since she'd left him, his own libido had gone into hibernation. From the feelings erupting through him now, he realised he'd shut down far more than his libido.

He'd shut down long before she'd left him.

Their marriage had begun with such high hopes and such certainty. They'd both been too foolish to realise that it was nothing but lust, a flaming passion that could only burn itself out.

He'd been intoxicated by her. He'd never met anyone like her: tough on the outside but marshmallow-soft inside. Straight talking. Capable of lancing with her tongue. But tender and compassionate. Someone who would drop everything if she were needed. Someone who would give everything they had if it were needed. Massimo had never been one for showing his emotions but being tactile with Livia had come naturally. She'd brought that side of him out right from the start.

And then the tide had turned. His assumptions that he would be able to continue his life and work in the same way he always had but with his beautiful, vivacious wife to come home to had been quickly dispelled.

He should never have married her, that was the truth of it, but he'd been so swept up in the need to tie her to him and make her his in every way possible that he'd blinded himself to what marriage to a woman like Livia would actually entail. It entailed far more than he could give.

* * *

It was still dark when Livia woke. Groping for her phone, she looked at the time and was relieved to see they only had a couple of hours left until they landed.

Creeping out of her bed so as not to wake Massimo, she took her overnight bag from the compartment and made her way to the bedroom. She needed a shower. It was pure misfortune that the main bathroom was reached through the bedroom.

The moment she opened the bedroom door and stepped inside, she realised her mistake. The bathroom light was already switched on and the scent of Massimo's shower gel seeped through the gap in the door. Before she could beat a hasty retreat, the door opened and he stepped over the threshold as naked as the day he was born.

Startled caramel eyes met hers. All the air flew from her lungs.

Seconds passed that stretched like hours as they did nothing but stare at each other.

A compression formed in her chest and tightened her throat.

For a man who rarely worked out, Massimo had a physique to die for. Lean but muscular, his deep olive skin had only the lightest brush of fine dark hair over his defined pecs and the plane of his washboard stomach. The hair thickened considerably below his abdomen to the huge…

Her own abdomen contracted, heat rushing through her pelvis as she noticed—couldn't *help* but notice—his growing erection.

The heat in her pelvis spread. It suffused her cheeks with colour and she tightened her hold on her bag, crushing it against her chest.

Slowly, his features became taut, his nostrils flaring. His caramel eyes swirled with something she recognised, something that should have her spinning round immediately and leaving. But she couldn't. Her feet were rooted to the floor.

He'd had more work done on his tattoo, she noticed dimly, trying desperately hard not to let her gaze fall back below his waist, trying even harder to contain the rush of sultry warmth flooding her veins. His tattoo covered the entire bicep around his left shoulder, all in bold black lines. The large sun, the centrepiece that he had once told her symbolised his rebirth and represented the way he strove for perfection in all he did, was encircled by sharks' teeth, which represented power, leadership and protection, and they were now encircled by spearheads. She didn't know what the spearheads represented but knew they must mean something to him.

Instinct told her they represented something to do with her.

The sensation in her fingers that had almost had her touching his sleeping face earlier tingled again. An ache to touch his tattoo. To touch him. A yearning to feel the heat of his powerful body flush against hers, to be swept in his arms and to lose herself in the wonder she had always found in his lovemaking. It all hit her so quickly that if he had reached out for her she would have fallen into his arms in an instant.

More seconds stretched without a word exchanged but with that thick, sick chemistry shrouding them.

And then Massimo closed his eyes.

When he next looked at her, the swirling desire had gone.

He'd shut down again.

He turned and walked back into the bathroom, locking the door behind him.

CHAPTER FOUR

LIVIA GAZED OUT of the window of the Cessna they'd transferred to after landing at Fiji's Nadi airport and soaked in the oval-shaped patch of land that rose like a majestic tropical oasis from the South Pacific below. Ringed with golden sand and light turquoise shores that deepened to ultramarine, Seibua Island was far more beautiful and exotic than even its namesake had described.

Livia had only ever travelled from her Italian homeland to the US; the scents that exploded through her airways when she stepped onto the small airfield were ones she'd never had the pleasure of smelling before.

She stared up at the rising sun before closing her eyes and savouring the sensation of the most incredible warmth on her skin.

Then she cast a glance at Massimo to witness his reaction at his first steps on his grand-father's homeland.

Far from savouring anything, he'd immediately headed to the waiting golf buggy and was introducing himself to its elderly driver.

Like Livia, who'd changed into a knee-length red sundress, Massimo had donned summer clothing too, opting for a pair of black canvas shorts and a fitted navy T-shirt with the cover of a hellraising rock band's album on it. Ever the chameleon, he looked as divine in these casual items as he did in a full dinner jacket but it only made her think that he never looked better than when he wore nothing at all, and she had to push hard to rid her mind of the vivid image of him standing before her naked. It was a battle she'd been losing for the past four hours.

She forced a smile at the two young men who were removing their luggage from the small plane and loading it onto a second buggy, and walked over to Massimo, who introduced her to the man he employed to run the island for him, first in English then in Italian for her benefit.

She shook the extended hand from the friendly looking man and carefully said, 'It is nice to see you.'

She caught the dart of surprise that flashed in Massimo's eyes but he said nothing about her attempt at English, indicating only that she should get into the buggy.

She slid into the back and was relieved when Massimo climbed in the front beside the driver.

'How long until we get to the complex?' she asked. The island was bigger than she'd envisaged. Naively, she'd imagined something around the size of a small field with a solitary palm tree as a marker.

'Not long. Five or ten minutes.'

Soon the thick, scented flora they drove through separated and the golden sand she'd seen from the air lay before them, glimmering under the glorious sunshine.

Stunned, she craned her neck to take in the thatched chalets nestled—but not too closely together—along the length of a high rock formation that ended on the shore of the beach. A long wooden bridge led the eye to a further thatched chalet that appeared to rise out of the ocean itself. On the other side of the thatched cottages and lower down, separated from the beach by a wall, lay the chalet designated for Massimo's grandfather. Beside it lay a handful of smaller though no less beautiful chalets. To the right of all these dwellings was the centrepiece, the huge, multi-purpose lodge behind which, virtually camouflaged by the coconut palms and other tropical trees and foliage that thrived on the island, were the structures that housed the great kitchens and the island staff's living quarters. Further to the right, where the beach curved out of sight, were the mangrove saplings, recently planted in their thousands to protect the island from erosion and rising sea levels.

Everything Massimo had envisaged for the island of his grandfather's birth had come to life in spectacular fashion.

The driver stopped in front of the main lodge and said something to Massimo before jumping out.

Livia's heart almost dropped to her feet when Massimo followed suit and held his hand out to her.

Confused at this unexpected gesture, especially since they'd spent the past four hours after she'd inadvertently walked in on him naked ignoring each other's existence, she stared into the caramel eyes that were fixed on her with an intensity that belied the easy smile playing on his lips.

A child's cry rang out and in an instant she understood. Massimo's family were already there. He was holding his hand out because they must be watching.

She reached out and wrapped her fingers loosely round the waiting hand.

At the first touch of her skin to his, her heart flew from her feet to her throat and her fingers reflexively tightened.

For that one singular moment in time, the world paused on its axis as she stared into his soulful eyes and a rush of helpless longing swept through her, long-buried emotions rising up and clutching her throat.

And then the ground beneath her feet began to spin.

These were emotions she'd buried for a reason—because they had never been returned with the same depth with which she'd held them.

Turning her head and blinking the brief spell away from her vision, she was thankful to see Madeline on the steps that led to the main entrance of the lodge holding her infant daughter, Elizabeth. Dropping Massimo's hand, Livia hurried over to them and embraced her sister-in-law, careful not to squash baby Elizabeth, who immediately grabbed at her hair.

Massimo watched his wife and sister's embrace, watched them exchange enthusiastic kisses, watched his wife rub a finger against his niece's chubby cheek before lifting the child into her own arms, and had to fight to keep a lid on the emotions threatening to overwhelm him.

Livia had laughed at his suggestion that they have a child.

Slowly he made his way towards them, bracing himself for the rebuke that was certain to be coming.

Madeline didn't disappoint. After the obligatory kisses, she took Elizabeth back from Livia and hitched her to her hip. 'Massimo, meet your niece, Elizabeth. Elizabeth, this is the uncle you've heard about who's been too busy saving the world to meet you.'

Were it not for the large blue eyes of his six-month-old niece staring at him with fascination, he would have sworn at his sister. 'It's been a long journey here. Can you save the harassment until I've said hello to everyone else?'

His sister smiled beadily. 'Sure. The others are in the lodge waiting for you.'

The others were, in fact, his grandfather and his army of carers, and Massimo and Madeline's parents. Tomorrow night his grandfather's surviving siblings and their spouses, children, grandchildren and great-grandchildren would either fly or sail to the island for the birthday party. It would be the first time his grandfather had seen all but one of his siblings since he'd left the island paradise, one of the remotest and smallest of all the Fijian islands, for Europe. He'd been the first Seibua to leave. In the almost seventy years since his emigration the rest of the Seibuas had, one by one, left the island of their birth too in search of better opportunities to raise their families. Most had settled on Fiji's largest island, Viti Levu. The soon-to-be renamed Seibua Island had been uninhabited for over a decade before Massimo had purchased it.

The main lodge was everything the architect had promised. Massimo had wanted a space large enough to accommodate the entire extended family, whether it was for a sit-down meal or a party, and it had been created accordingly. Dining tables lined the walls to the left, plush sofas lined the walls to the right. A bar ran the length of the far wall. The space in between was large enough for a hundred people to dance or for an army of children to skid on and scuff the expensive flooring. He estimated that tomorrow evening there would be a minimum of fifteen children there to test it out.

For now, though, it was only immediate family there and the knotted weight of expectation that came with being them. Massimo hadn't seen any of them in over a year. But Livia had, and he watched her embrace his parents as if she were the child of their loins and not a mere daughter-in-law. She had never understood where his ambivalence to his family had come from. In his wife's eyes, he'd been raised with everything she'd wanted and been denied.

Livia's childhood had been torrid; filled with violence and menace, her father murdered before she reached double digits, her mother the manager of a wedding dress shop who sold drugs for extra cash along with the white lace creations. Her mother also received a monthly payment from Don Fortunato, the mafia boss Livia's father had protected. Blood money, Livia always disdainfully referred to it as. Money had never been an issue in the Esposito home. She'd told Massimo once of going into the back storeroom of her mother's shop and finding wads of cash wrapped in elastic bands in one of the boxes that was supposed to store garter belts. She'd estimated it at half a million euros. Money that belonged to Don Fortunato, stashed away until he came to reclaim it and launder it back into the world.

It had taken more guts than Massimo could comprehend for Livia to claw her way out of that violent, narcotic-infested world. She saw his childhood as idyllic, had no comprehension of what it was like to walk rain-lashed streets with holes in the soles of her shoes or to be the butt of school tormentors' jokes because the clothes you wore were two sizes too small and threadbare. He could have coped with being the butt of all the jokes if his parents had worked hard, as his one close friend's parents had, the father holding down two jobs, the mother working school hours, but they didn't. They hadn't. His father had worked in a shoe repair shop. By mutual agreement, his mother hadn't worked since Massimo's birth.

Life was for living! his father would proudly proclaim. Not for being a slave!

What did it matter if they could only afford to eat meat once a week? Their vegetable patch grew an abundance of nutritious food!

What did it matter if they couldn't afford to buy Massimo a new calculator when his was flushed down the toilet by his school tormentors? His brain was advanced enough to be its own calculator!

His brain was advanced enough to be its own calculator out of necessity, not design.

And it had been advanced enough to know that if he wanted to make anything of his life it would have to come from him alone. From the age of thirteen, he'd worked for anyone who would employ him: running errands, stacking shelves, working on market stalls, cleaning offices. You name it, he'd done it. He'd bought his own computer and a phone, the rest of the money he'd stashed away for university, which was just as well as when it had come time for him to leave home for the wonder that was higher education, his parents had not had a single cent spare to help him.

It was during his university years that he'd created the platform game that had made him his initial fortune and also brought him closer to his grandparents. They'd moved to Rome when their daughter had married Massimo's Italian father and, their apartment being much closer to his university than his parents' home, had insisted he visit regularly for home-cooked food and a comfortable bed. It was in these years that he'd learned more about his grandfather's roots and heritage.

And now he was here in the place he'd visited only in his imagination, about to be closeted with his family for the first time in two years.

His parents' eyes were alight as he approached them.

What he intended to be a sedate, functional greeting was quickly turned into a greeting worthy of Hollywood. His father ignored his outstretched hand and pulled him into an embrace that would have squeezed the life out of a weaker man, then his mother did the same. Their exuberantly delivered words were lost amidst the planting of paternal and maternal kisses all over his face.

When he was finally able to disentangle himself, he turned to greet his grandfather and found himself faltering.

The wizened man sitting in a wheelchair with an oxygen tank attached…that was his grandfather? This was Jimmy Seibua?

Getting down to his haunches, Massimo stared into the filmy eyes that had once been the darkest chocolate then gently embraced him, his heart pounding with shock and pain.

It was like embracing a skeleton.

He hid his shock with the widest smile he could conjure. From the periphery of his vision he saw Livia speaking to one of his grandfather's medical team. He would talk to them too. Soon. When he was confident he could speak without ripping their heads off.

Soon the entire family was reclining together on sofas dragged together to form a square, his grandfather wheeled over to be with them, fresh coffee, pastries and fruit brought out for them to devour.

This should be a moment of great satisfaction for him but instead Massimo felt as if he'd been hit by an articulated lorry. His chest felt tight, as if all the air had been sucked out and his lungs and heart vacuum packed. He detested small talk at the best of times but right then he could hardly move his tongue to form simple words, responding to his brother-in-law's chat with grunts and monosyllables.

At his sister's instigation, he'd arranged for them to spend the day on the yacht he'd bought for the island, sailing out to a tiny atoll twenty kilometres away. This atoll was circled by a protected coral reef even more spectacular than the one surrounding Seibua Island and which cruise liners were forbidden from visiting.

Only another forty-eight hours to go until he could leave and return to his home and work in America.

He had a feeling these were going to be the longest forty-eight hours of his life. The distance between them had never felt greater. This was his family but he'd never felt a part of it. Part of *them*. Always he'd felt like the cuckoo in the nest. If he didn't have such a strong physical resemblance to his father and the colouring of his mother, he could easily believe he'd been adopted.

The only person he'd ever felt completely at ease with had been Livia but he now knew the ease had been a dopamine-induced illusion. She was sitting on the opposite sofa chatting to Madeline with baby Elizabeth on her lap, uncaring that her hair was being pulled by a tight, pudgy fist.

His estranged wife was more comfortable with his family than he was. The woman who'd laughed at having a child with him was laughing now, pretty white teeth gleaming where the sun's rays filtered through the high windows and bathed her in their light.

It was only when their eyes met that he saw the effort it was costing her to maintain a care-free front. When he'd walked out of his bath-room naked and found her standing there...

He'd wanted to touch her with an ache that came from the very centre of his being.

The desire he'd thought had died with their marriage had come back to life as if it had never left. Livia still breathed in his blood. She pumped through his veins in a hot, relentless motion that seeped through his every pore, making his skin feverish.

There could be no going back. She was only there because of her love for his grandfather and her affection for the rest of his family.

Massimo waited until he'd drained his cof-fee before getting to his feet. 'I need to stretch my legs,' he announced. 'I'll see you all on the yacht in an hour.' Without waiting for a response, he strode out of the lodge and into the blazing sun.

His chalet was the one over the bridge and

he headed towards it without breaking stride. His family didn't need him to entertain them. They were already settled in and relaxed in their surroundings, already tanned and glowing. All except his grandfather...

'Massimo, will you *wait*?'

Muttering a curse under his breath, he turned his head. Livia was hurrying in his direction, her hair flowing in a stream behind her.

'Problem?' he asked tightly when she reached him.

Livia snatched a breath of air. It had been years since she'd walked so quickly. 'I was going to ask you the same thing.'

His family had all turned their questioning eyes to her when he'd left the lodge. She'd shrugged apologetically and murmured that it had been a long flight before following him out.

He grunted and set off again.

'Are you going to tell me what's on your mind?' she asked when she caught up with him. Her short legs made double his strides to keep pace.

'I'm going to call the owner of the agency.'

'What agency?'

'The one who supplied the nurses and carers who were supposed to look after my grandfather. The agency *you* used to work for.'

They both stepped onto the wooden bridge without changing pace. It felt as substantial beneath her feet as the earth itself. 'Why?'

'I chose that agency because my previous experience with them was positive. I am disgusted that they've allowed him to get into this state. He's skin and bone. When was the last time he had a shave? My grandfather has shaved every day of his adult life and now he looks like a homeless drug addict.'

They'd reached the door to their cabin but before he could open it, Livia placed a hand on his wrist.

'I tried to warn you,' she said gently when he finally met her gaze. A pulse throbbed in his jaw.

He closed his eyes then shook her hand away. 'I know his cancer is incurable,' he bit out. 'That is no excuse for allowing him to get in such a state.'

She sighed and followed him into the chalet. After closing the door, she rested her back against it and tried to think of the words to use that wouldn't add to his distress. For she was quite certain that his anger was nothing but a mask for his anguish at seeing first-hand how close to death his grandfather really was.

'He's lost so much weight because he can't handle solid food any more,' she told him quietly. 'They can't shave him as often as he would like because his skin's become too sensitive. He can only cope with them doing it once a week.'

'You would make excuses for them,' he retorted scathingly. 'The medical profession always protects its own.'

'Even if I was still on the agency's books I wouldn't make excuses for medical negligence.'

The usually soulful eyes glittered menacingly. 'You accept they've neglected him?'

'No. They have given him exceptional care. The problem is it's been so long since you last saw Jimmy that the changes are more obvious to you.'

'I knew it wouldn't take long for you to get around to *my* supposed neglect of him.'

Livia sighed again in lieu of biting her tongue and in a vain effort to temper the anger rising in her. This was a weekend for celebration, not recriminations. Massimo was the one who had to live with his conscience, not her.

'Your grandfather is very ill, Massimo, but he's as comfortable and as pain-free as he can be. He's here on the island he loves with the family he loves. *You* made this happen, all of it. Don't spoil things for him by taking your anger at his condition out on those who have done their best for him.'

His jaw tightened as she spoke. For a long time he didn't respond, just stared at her until his nostrils flared and he gave a sharp nod. 'I need to call in with the office.'

This time her sigh was one of exasperation.

'I need to answer any questions the project manager has about the analysis and data before we set sail. Okay?'

She was glad he turned his back on her and strode through to the chalet's living room, his wretched phone already in his hand. It meant he didn't see the sheen of tears that suddenly filled her eyes.

CHAPTER FIVE

LIVIA TAMPED DOWN the gulf of feelings knotting her belly and boarded the white yacht. Although dwarfed in size by the cruise ship it was moored next to, it still dazzled with elegance. After their mammoth journey to the island she would have preferred to spend the day relaxing but this was the trip Madeline had forced Massimo to concede to. Livia knew what her sister-in-law was thinking: that forcing Massimo into close quarters would stop him hiding away.

Unfortunately, Madeline hadn't reckoned on Massimo boarding the yacht with his laptop case slung over his shoulder and his phone sticking out of his shorts pocket and Livia saw her lips pull in tightly. When they set sail, Livia was the only one secretly pleased when he made his excuses and disappeared inside.

Disappointment was writ large on his family's faces.

She met Madeline's gaze and shrugged apologetically.

Barely three hours with Massimo's family and she'd already made two silent apologies for him.

Sailing at a steady pace over the calm South Pacific, it took only an hour to reach the atoll. They whiled the time away in a lazy fashion, dipping in and out of the swimming pool and chatting. The captain anchored the yacht at a distance far enough away not to cause any damage to the precious reef but close enough for them all to see the clear turquoise water teeming with brightly coloured fish and all other manner of sea life. Madeline and Raul donned their snorkelling gear and jumped in, leaving baby Elizabeth in Sera's capable hands.

Livia looked out at Madeline and Raul having the time of their lives in the water, at Sera playing happily with her granddaughter, at her father-in-law Gianni, book in one hand, large cocktail in the other, at Jimmy napping in his wheelchair in a shaded part of the deck, at the chefs cooking up a storm on the barbecue and felt a sharp pang rip through her chest.

Massimo should be there with them.

She hurried down the stairs and slipped inside in search of him.

The interior of the yacht was vast and as sleek and as elegant as the exterior and refreshingly cool after the hazy heat on deck. It took a few minutes before she found him hidden in an isolated section of the saloon, tapping away on his laptop. So engrossed was he in his work that it took a few moments before he noticed her presence.

'Lunch is almost ready,' she said briskly.

'I'll be ten minutes.'

'And then you'll turn your laptop off and leave it off?'

'I can't.'

She inhaled deeply to smother her anger. 'Your family have been looking forward to spending time with you.'

'And they will.'

'When?' she challenged. 'Tomorrow, everything will be about the party and then you go back to LA. Today is the only day when it's just us and you're missing out. You've travelled thousands of kilometres to be here. It's not going to kill you to turn your laptop off and spend some time with your family.'

His jaw clenched, his fingers now drumming on the table rather than tapping on his laptop.

Looking at the obstinate set of Livia's jawline, Massimo knew she wouldn't give him a moment's peace until he joined the rest of them on deck.

It wasn't that he disliked spending time with his family. Not really. It was that they were all so different from him. His approach to life was alien to them. They believed he worked too hard, never understanding that it was only when he was immersed in his work that he felt at peace with himself.

It would be easier to handle these few days with them if Livia weren't there. It was hard enough dealing with his family's suffocating love without adding his estranged wife and all the intense emotions she'd drawn back out of him into the mix.

How could he find ease in her company when his attention was consumed by her every movement? She stood a good five feet from him but awareness thrummed through him, a buzz on his skin, an itch in his fingers. Her black swimsuit was designed for functionality and not for flaunting her body but still he reacted as if she were wearing the skimpiest of bikinis. The itch in his fingers became unbearable when he noticed the smudge of mascara under her left eye from where she'd dried her face after her swim. He wanted to rub the smudge away.

He breathed in deeply through his nose and nodded. 'I'll turn my laptop off and join you in ten minutes.'

She inclined her head and backed away. Just when he thought he was rid of her she fixed him with a hard stare counteracted by a quirking at the corner of her lips. 'If you get your phone out at all while we're on this yacht, I can't promise that it won't become fish food.'

Two hours later and Livia almost wished Massimo would return to the saloon and do more work.

After they'd eaten their long lunch; barbecued fish freshly caught that morning and an array of salads, she'd gone snorkelling with Madeline and climbed back on board to find Massimo had removed his T-shirt and draped it carelessly on the back of his chair.

Trying hard to blur his magnificent physique from her sight, she wrapped her beach towel around her waist while Madeline went straight to Raul, wrapped her arms around his neck and kissed the top of his balding head. In response, he twisted in his chair and squeezed her bottom.

Livia couldn't stop her eyes from seeking Massimo, her heart throbbing as she remembered a time when they'd been as tactile and affectionate together as his sister and brother-in-law were. Her insides heated to match the warmth on her skin when she found his gaze already on her. Was he remembering those heady, carefree days too…?

His eyes pulsed before he looked away and reached for the jug of fruit cocktail. He refilled his glass then filled another and pulled out the empty chair beside him. Livia sat, accepting the drink with a murmured thanks, and tried again to blur out his naked chest. Even with the parasol raised to shade them from the worst of the heat, the sun's rays were slow-roasting them. One of Jimmy's carers had taken him inside for a nap.

Madeline pulled a bottle of sunscreen from her bag. Once she and Raul had slathered themselves in it, she passed the bottle to Livia, who rubbed the lotion over her face, covered her arms, shoulders, the top part of her chest not covered by her swimsuit and her neck. But she couldn't reach all of her back.

'Here, let me.'

Of course Massimo would offer to help. They had a watching audience, just as they'd had when they'd arrived at the lodge and he'd offered his hand to help her out of the golf buggy. His offer was for their benefit. If not for them, he would probably let her burn.

Trying valiantly to keep her features nonchalant, Livia gave the bottle to Massimo and twisted in her seat so her back was to him.

The anticipation of his touch was almost unbearable. And when it came...

Her breath caught in her throat.

Darts of awareness spread through her, memories flooding her of the first time he'd applied sunscreen to her skin. They'd been on their honeymoon in St Barts. They'd sunbathed naked, secure in their privacy. Massimo had rubbed the lotion sensually over every inch of her skin. By the time he'd rolled her onto her back and driven deep inside her, she'd been wet and aching for him. It had been the quickest she had ever achieved orgasm.

Now, he applied the lotion to her back briskly. His indifference made her heart twist with sadness but she worked hard to keep her lips curved upwards.

His hands pulled away with an abruptness that made the twist in her heart turn to an ache.

'Turn around and I'll do your back,' she ordered, proud that her voice was as bright as she intended for their watching audience.

As he was so tall and broad, there was a lot more skin to cover than the small area of exposed flesh on her own back.

Resisting the temptation to squirt it straight onto his back and have the fleeting enjoyment of watching him squirm at the quick shock of cold on his warm skin, she placed a healthy dollop into her palm, rubbed her hands together to spread it equally between them then placed them on his shoulder blades.

He still flinched.

She worked as briskly as he had to rub the lotion into his smooth skin.

When had she last touched his back? She couldn't remember. The coldness that had entered their marriage hadn't appeared overnight. It had accumulated over time until one day there was nothing but ice where once there had been love.

She had forgotten how much pleasure she got from simply touching him. Massimo carried so much on his shoulders. She'd loved to massage his knots away and feel him relax beneath her fingers. There were knots there now beneath the pads of her fingers, at the top of his spine and around his shoulder blades. Big ones.

Livia gritted her teeth and, dragging her hands from the knotted shoulders, swept down to the base of his back and covered the last bit that needed protection from the blazing sun.

The weight on his shoulders and the knots formed by it were none of her concern.

The moment she was done she pulled her hands away with the same abruptness that he'd done with her then breathed a quick sigh of relief when the captain appeared on deck, distracting everyone's attention. It was time to sail back.

His family's natural exuberance, which Massimo had never inherited, made sailing a noisy affair. The three women were in the pool swimming with his niece, laughing and splashing, leaving him at the table with his father, grandfather and brother-in-law, answering questions as best he could about the carbon filter he was days away from testing the prototype of. He could see the effort it was taking for them to concentrate.

He couldn't help his gaze drifting to the swimming pool, his attention as attuned as it had always been to Livia's every movement.

He was also intensely aware that she'd left

her phone on the table and intensely ashamed that he wanted to snatch it up, take it somewhere private and trawl through all her communications over the past four months. He wondered how she would react if he were to throw it overboard and give it the same fate she'd threatened his own phone.

As if it were aware of his attention, her phone suddenly burst into life.

His father peered at it. 'Livia, Gianluca's calling,' he called to her.

'Coming!' She scrambled out of the pool, snatching her towel as she padded to the table, but her brother's call had gone to voicemail before she reached them.

Her brow furrowed. 'Excuse me a moment. I need to call him back.'

As she climbed the stairs to the top deck, Massimo's mother got out of the pool and joined them at the table.

'How is Gianluca doing?' she asked him in an undertone, concern writ large on her face. 'I know Livia has been very worried about him.'

But he never got the chance to ask what she was talking about for Madeline had sneaked up behind him and suddenly thrust a soaking Elizabeth into his arms. 'Here you go, Massimo. You can hold Elizabeth for me.'

'Where are you going?'

'Nowhere.' She stood at the balustrade with a cackle of laughter that produced laughs from his parents and a sound that could have been laughter too from his grandfather.

With a wriggling baby thrust upon him, Massimo filed away his mother's comment about Livia's youngest sibling as something to query later. Gianluca was the only member of Livia's family he'd met. He'd turned up at their wedding looking furtive, constantly looking over his shoulder. His behaviour, Livia had later explained, was a mirror of her own when she'd first left Naples, a habit it had taken her years to break.

He hoped Gianluca hadn't finally fallen into the life Livia had escaped from and which she'd so dearly hoped he would follow her out of.

Teenage boys were pack animals. That was Livia's theory for why he hadn't attempted to escape yet. He went around the Secondigliano with his gang of friends on their scooters, chasing girls, playing video games, employed by the brutal men who ran the territory to keep watch for enemies and the police. Livia was convinced that it was a life her brother didn't want but Massimo was equally convinced that Gianluca had been as seduced by it as the rest of her family had been and that sooner or later he would be seduced into committing a crime from which there would be no going back. Livia's strength of mind and moral code were rare.

He stood his niece on his lap and stared at her cherubic face and felt the tightness in his chest loosen. This little one would be raised with security and love. She would never be exposed to the danger and violence his wife and her siblings had lived.

Huge blue eyes stared back. Unable to resist, he sniffed the top of her head. She smelled of baby.

'When are you two going to have one of those?' Raul asked with a grin.

Ice laced like a snake up Massimo's spine in an instant.

All eyes focused on him...and the presence

he sensed behind him. Livia had returned from her phone call.

She sat back down, phone clutched in her hand. 'It's not the right time for us to have a child,' she said and shrugged apologetically. 'You know the hours Massimo puts into his work.'

'You would work those hours if there was a child?' his mother said, looking at him with an air of bewilderment. It was a look he'd become used to during his childhood, a physical expression that the differences between Massimo and his family were felt as keenly by them as they were by him.

'My work is important,' he pointed out cordially. He didn't expect her to understand. To his parents, work was only important in as much as it paid the bills. That hadn't stopped his parents from accepting the luxury home he'd purchased for them and for which he footed all the bills *and* the monthly sum he transferred into their bank account for everything else they could possibly need. He did the same for his sister and his grandfather and for his father's siblings and their offspring. He would have done the same for his mother's siblings if she'd had any.

He had stopped them ever having to work again—work being something none of the extended Briatores had been enamoured with either—and still his work ethic bewildered them. He provided for them all and the source of their wealth came from the technology he was creating that would, hopefully, allow baby Elizabeth, along with future generations of Briatores, to live on a planet that wasn't a raging fireball. And still they stared at him with bewilderment, unable to comprehend why he worked as hard as he did.

'I know, but…' His mother must have sensed something from his expression for her voice trailed off.

Livia had no such sensibilities. Pouring herself a glass of fruit cocktail, she said, 'Your son is a workaholic, Sera. It makes for a lonely life for me. I could not bring a child into that.'

'You could get help,' his mother suggested hopefully.

Livia shook her head. 'In America, any help would be from English speakers. I've been trying to learn but it's very hard. I had a cut on my leg last year that needed stitching and it was very stressful trying to understand the staff at the hospital.'

Talk of that incident made Massimo's guts clench uncomfortably and his gaze automatically drift down to her leg. The scar, although expertly stitched and incredibly neat, was still vivid. Livia had gone for a swim in their outdoor pool in LA. One of the pebbled tiles around its perimeter had broken away leaving a sharp edge that she had sliced her calf on when hauling herself out of the pool. He'd been at his testing facility when she'd called to tell him about it, saying only that she'd cut her leg and needed help communicating with a medical practitioner about it. He'd sent Lindy, fluent in Italian, to deal with it and translate for her.

He'd been furious when he'd returned home that night and seen the extent of the damage. Seventeen stitches, internal and external. Her reply had been the coolest he'd ever received from her—up to that point anyway—Livia saying, 'I didn't want to make a drama out of it and worry you while you were driving.' He'd stared at her quizzically. Her lips had tightened. 'I assumed you would come.'

It wasn't his fault, he told himself stubbornly. He wasn't a mind reader. He couldn't have known how bad the damage had been.

The damage it had caused to their marriage in the longer term had been far more extensive.

'Look!' His sister's exclamation cut through his moody reminiscences.

Everyone followed Madeline's pointed finger. Holding Elizabeth securely in his arms, Massimo carried her to the balustrade. Swimming beside the yacht, almost racing them, was a pod of bottlenose dolphins.

Around thirty of the beautiful mammals sped sleekly through the water, creating huge white foams with their dives. It was as if they'd come to check them out and decided to stay for a while and play.

It was one of the most incredible sights he had ever seen and it filled him with something indefinable; indefinable because it was nothing he'd ever felt before.

He looked at Livia and the awed joy on her

face and experienced a fleeting gratitude that she'd forced him from his work and enabled him to enjoy this priceless moment.

Elizabeth wriggled in his arms. He tightened his hold on her to stop her falling and, as he did, Livia's blame as to their childless state came back to him and the brief lightness that had filled his chest leached back out.

Livia tried her hardest to keep a happy front going but it only got harder as time passed. Gianluca hadn't answered her returned call and he hadn't called or left a message since.

And then there was Massimo.

The excitement of the dolphins racing so joyously alongside them had waned once they'd finally swum off and the lightness she'd witnessed in his eyes had quickly waned too. Was she the only one to notice his underlying tension? She would bet the knots on his shoulders had become even tighter.

Her assumption that he would keep the reasons for his anger to himself was dispelled when they returned to the island. His family retired to their chalets for a late siesta before dinner, leaving them together on the terrace of the lodge drinking a coconut and rum creation the head bar steward had made for them.

The moment they were alone, he fixed her with hard eyes. 'Why did you say all that rubbish about a baby?'

'What rubbish?'

'You let my family believe the issue of us not having children lies with me.'

'I'm prepared to pretend that our marriage is intact but I'm not prepared to tell an outright lie.'

'You're the one who didn't want a child. Not me.'

Confused, she blinked. 'When did I say I didn't want a child?'

His jaw clenched. 'You laughed when I suggested we have one.'

'Do you mean the time you suggested we have a child to cure me of my loneliness? Is that the time you're referring to?' Of course it was. It was the only time the subject of a baby had come up since their first heady days when they'd spoken of a future that involved children. 'I laughed at the suggestion, yes, because it *was* laughable. And even if you hadn't suggested a child as a sticking plaster for my loneliness I would still have laughed and for the reasons I shared with your mother—ours was no marriage to bring a child into.'

His hand tightened perceptibly around his glass. 'You made it sound like you're a neglected wife.'

'I *was* a neglected wife,' she bit back. 'Why do you think I left you? To pretend otherwise is demeaning—'

'You're here this weekend so my grandfather can spend what is likely to be his last birthday on this earth believing everything is fine between us,' he interrupted.

'We're not going to do that by pretending that you've suddenly turned into a model husband, are we? Your grandfather isn't stupid—none of your family are, and they're not going to believe a leopard can change its spots. I visited your family on my own and made excuses for you for over a year before I left and I've been doing the same for the last four months and they have been none the wiser about the state of our marriage. When we finally come clean that we've separated, the only surprise will be that it's taken me so long to see sense.'

Livia knew she was baiting him but she didn't care. She wanted him to argue with her. She'd always wanted him to argue back but he never did. It was a circle that had only grown more vicious as their marriage limped on; her shouting, him clamming up.

True to form, Massimo's mouth clamped into a straight line. He pushed his chair back roughly and got to his feet but before he could stride away as she fully expected him to do, he turned back around and glowered at her. 'Unless you want a fight over any divorce settlement, I suggest you stick to the plan and stop putting doubts about our marriage in my family's head. I don't care what my parents or sister think but I will not have my grandfather having doubts about us.'

'If you want a fight over the settlement then I'll give you a fight,' she said, outraged at his threat, 'but I *am* sticking to the plan! You've neglected your family for so long that they think it's normal that you neglect your wife too.'

'I'm not having this argument again.'

She laughed bitterly. Her hands were shaking. 'We never argued about it. Whenever I tried to tell you how unhappy I was, you walked away from me. You never wanted to hear it.'

'You were like a stuck record.' He made crablike pinching motions with his hands. 'I'm bored, Massimo,' he mimicked. 'I'm lonely, Massimo. Why do you work such long hours, Massimo?' He dropped his hands and expelled his own bitter laugh. 'See? I *did* listen. Maybe if you'd ever paused for breath between complaints I might have felt more incentivised to come home earlier each night.'

'I only complained *because* you work such stupid hours!'

His eyes were cold. 'I didn't force you to move to America. I didn't force you to marry me. You knew the kind of man I was before we married but you thought you could change me. Instead of solving your problems for yourself you sat around the house wallowing and complaining and expecting me to fix everything for you.'

'I never wallowed!' she said, outraged. Of all

the things he'd just accused her of, for some reason that was the one that immediately bit the hardest. 'And as if I would have expected you to fix anything—you aren't capable of fixing anything to do with the human heart. You've spent so much time with your machines and gadgets that your heart has turned to metal.'

He took the three steps needed to smile cruelly down at her. 'You did nothing *but* wallow. And sulk. And complain. For the first few weeks after you left I thought I'd gone deaf.'

And then his smile turned into a grimace as he turned on his heel and, parting shot delivered, strode off leaving Livia standing there feeling as if he'd just ripped her heart out.

CHAPTER SIX

MASSIMO LOCKED THE bathroom door. He didn't trust Livia not to barge in.

He'd expected her to follow him to the chalet. Every step had been taken with an ear braced for a fresh verbal assault.

But the assault never came.

He turned the shower on and closed his eyes to the hot water spraying over his head.

Livia's defiant yet stricken face played in his retinas.

Guilt fisted his guts. He'd been cruel. The words had spilled out of him as if a snake had taken possession of his tongue.

Being here…with Livia, with his family, seeing how close to death his grandfather really was…it was all too much.

Hearing accusations of neglectful behaviour towards those he loved had driven like a knife in his heart.

He'd done his best for his family. They might not see him as much as they would like but he made up for his lack of presence in other ways.

And he'd done his best in his marriage. That his best did not live up to his wife's exacting standards was not his fault. Neglect seemed to suggest that she was a child who needed taking care of when they both knew Livia was more than capable of taking care of herself. This was the woman who'd survived the Secondigliano without being seduced by its violent glamour. This was the woman who'd discovered an affinity for nursing when the local doctor the neighbourhood gangsters visited to fix their gangland wounds recognised her coolness under pressure when one of her cousins got shot in the leg. From the age of fourteen Livia had been paid a flat fee of fifty euros a time to assist the doctor whenever required. Like Massimo, she'd stashed it away. Unlike Massimo, who'd saved his money in a box in his bedroom, never having to worry about his family stealing it from him, she'd kept her cash in a waterproof container under the vase in her father's grave. As she was the only mourner to place flowers on the grave, it was the only safe place she had for it.

She'd refused to be sucked into a life of crime. The only vice she'd picked up in her years where drugs were cheap and plentiful was cigarette smoking, which she'd quit when she'd achieved the grades needed to study nursing in Rome and taken all her cash and left the life behind her. She was as tough as nails. To suggest she needed caring for was laughable.

Finished showering, he rubbed his body with a towel then wrapped it around his waist. Bracing himself, he unlocked the door and stepped into the bedroom.

He'd been right to brace himself. Livia was sitting on the end of the bed waiting for him. But the fury he expected to be met with was nowhere to be seen. Her eyes, when he met them, were sad. The smudge of mascara was still visible.

After a moment's silence that felt strangely melancholic, she said, 'I don't want it to be like this.' It was the quietest he'd ever heard her speak.

He ran a hand through his damp hair and grimaced. 'I thought you wanted me to argue with you. Isn't that what you've always said?'

'Arguing's healthy, but this…?' Her shoulders and chest rose before slumping sharply, her gaze falling to the floor. 'I don't want us to be cruel to each other. I knew things would be difficult this weekend but…' Her voice trailed away before she slowly raised her head to meet his gaze. There was a sheen in her eyes that made his heart clench. 'This is much harder than I thought it would be.'

Massimo pressed his back against the bathroom door and closed his eyes. 'It's harder than I thought it would be too.'

'It is?'

He nodded and ground his teeth together. 'I shouldn't have said the things I said. I'm sorry.'

'I didn't know you felt like that.'

'I don't.' At her raised, disbelieving brow, he added, 'Not in the way I said it.'

'You made me sound like a fishwife.'

His lips curved involuntarily at the glimmer of humour in her tone. 'I was lashing out.

Being with you…' The fleeting smile faded away. 'I can't explain how it makes me feel.'

'It just makes me feel sad,' she admitted with a whisper. Then she rubbed her eyes with the palms of her hands and took a deep breath. 'When the time is right for us to file the divorce papers, I won't be wanting a settlement.'

'I didn't mean it about fighting you. We can come to an—'

Her head shook. 'No. No settlement. You've given me enough money since we married. I've hardly spent any of it. I've enough to buy an apartment—'

'You were going to buy one when you went back to Rome,' he interrupted. 'You were supposed to let my lawyer know when you'd found somewhere.' He'd informed his lawyer and accountant that Livia would be purchasing a home in Italy in her sole name and that funds should be made available to her when she got in touch with them about it, no questions asked. He didn't care what she spent.

He'd specifically told them to go ahead without notifying him. He hadn't wanted to know when she'd made that last, permanent move out of his life for reasons he couldn't explain, not even to himself.

Massimo ran his eyes over his finances once a year when it was tax season and that was for scrutiny purposes. He would have noticed then, he supposed, that she hadn't bought herself a home.

'I've been renting my old place.' Actually buying herself a home of her own had felt too final, Livia realised. It would have been the ultimate confirmation that their marriage was over for good.

Had she been living in denial? And if so, what had she been holding out for? Miracles didn't exist. The cruel truth was that she and Massimo were wholly incompatible and she'd been a fool for believing differently. She'd known it when she'd left. It hadn't stopped her heart skipping every time her phone had buzzed only to plummet when his name didn't flash on the screen. It hadn't flashed once since their separation.

'Once everything's out in the open, I'm going to go back to nursing,' she added, fighting back a well of tears. To cry in front of him would be the final indignity.

He rested his head back against the bathroom door with a sigh. 'You don't need to work, Liv.'

The simple shortening of her name…oh, but it made her heart *ache*. Massimo was the only person in the world who'd ever shortened her name. And then he'd stopped calling her Liv and started calling her Livia like everyone else. And then he'd stopped calling her anything.

Blinking away the tears that were still desperately trying to unleash, she sniffed delicately and gave a jerky nod. 'I need a sense of purpose. I like knowing the money in my pocket is earned by my own endeavours. I never wanted to be a kept woman.'

His throat moved before he gave his own nod. 'At least let me buy you a home like we agreed I would. The law entitles you to much more.'

And he would give it, everything the law said she was entitled to and more. If only he were as generous with his time as he was with his money...

But those were pointless thoughts to have. Massimo was who he was, just as Livia was who she was. They'd tried. They'd failed.

She just wished she could find a way to stop her heart from hurting so much.

'Thank you.' Swallowing hard to dislodge the lump in her throat, she got to her feet. 'I'll leave you to get changed. I'm going to make myself a coffee—would you like one?'

'That would be great, thank you.'

She smiled and left the bedroom and kept smiling as she made the coffee, smiling so hard that eventually the tears sucked themselves dry and her cheeks ached miserably in their place.

It didn't occur to her until she was standing under the shower an hour later that this was the first real conversation she and Massimo had had that hadn't descended to insults and recriminations in over a year.

The cloudless sky had turned deep blue, the sun a deep orange shimmering on the horizon when Livia ventured out of the chalet in search of Massimo. She found him on the wrap-around veranda drinking a bottle of beer and looking at his phone, wearing a pair of old battered jeans and a crisp white shirt, a booted foot hooked casually on his thigh.

It was the first time she'd been at the rear of their chalet and she tried hard not to let sadness fill her as she recalled poring over the architect's designs for it, imagining all the happy times she and Massimo would spend here. This chalet had been the only part of the complex Massimo had taken a real interest in. They'd chosen to build it high on the jutting mound of earth that, when the tide was low, could be walked to along a sandy pathway created by nature at its finest. This was supposed to be their own private hideaway in their private paradise. Their horseshoe swimming pool, garden and veranda were entirely hidden from prying eyes.

She hadn't been able to bring herself to think about the sleeping arrangements that night. Their chalet only had one bed. It was a huge bed but, still, it was only the one bed. She supposed she could sleep on the sofa. Massimo's long frame would never fit on it.

His eyes widened slightly when he looked up as she approached and he unhooked his foot and straightened.

The vain part of her bloomed to see his response. Although it was only a family meal they were going to have, she'd applied her make-up and done her hair with care. She'd been mortified to look in the mirror and see a huge smudge of mascara under her left eye.

But it wasn't vanity that had propelled her to make an effort. It was armoury. When she looked her best it had the effect of boosting her morale and for all the unspoken truce they'd forged, her emotions were all over the place. She needed every piece of armour she could find to hold herself together.

Massimo turned his phone off and tried hard to temper the emotions crashing through him. Livia had dressed casually in a pair of tight white three-quarter-length trousers and a shimmering red strappy top that stopped at her midriff. On her feet were high, white strappy sandals that elongated her frame but did nothing to diminish her natural curves.

A lifetime ago he would have beckoned her over, put his hands on her hips and pulled her to him.

The instant awakening of his loins proved, as if it needed proving, that nothing had changed. He still wanted her with an ache he felt deep in his marrow.

Inhaling deeply through his nose, he willed the thudding of his heart to steady.

'You're ready?' he asked.

She nodded.

He finished his beer and got to his feet.

In silence they walked the veranda to the front of the chalet and headed to the lodge. The tide had risen in the past two hours, the sandy path now mostly submerged beneath the powerful ocean and the colourful, tropical fish that swam in it. Its gentle rhythm was soothing.

His family had beaten them to the lodge and were all sitting around a set dining table chatting noisily. One of his grandfather's carers sat discreetly in a far corner of the lodge reading a book.

The meal passed quickly. His grandfather was tired and, fed by Massimo's mother, ate only his soup before retiring for the night. Madeline and Raul quickly followed, taking an increasingly fractious Elizabeth, who'd turned her nose up at all the offerings they'd tried to tempt her with. Considering it looked like mushed vomit, Massimo didn't blame her for smacking the plastic spoon out of her mother's hand. When his brother-in-law attempted to feed her, her little face turned bright red with fury. If Massimo had been offered that excuse for food, he'd have been tempted to screw his face up and bawl too.

He was about to rise and retire to the chalet to check in on work, when his father's suggestion of a game of Scopa, the traditional Italian game played with an Italian forty-card deck, gave him pause.

His mother's hopeful gaze made his ready refusal stick on his tongue before he could vocalise it.

He didn't need to look at Livia to know she was beseeching him with her eyes to accept too. Her earlier insistence that his family wanted only to spend time with him kept ringing in his ears.

He stretched his mouth into the semblance of a smile. 'Sure.'

The beaming grins made his chest tighten.

He signalled to the barman. Soon, a bottle of bourbon, a bucket of ice and four glasses had been taken to the outside table they now sat around. Massimo and his father formed a team and sat opposite each other, the ladies playing as the opposing team. Livia sat beside his father, his mother beside Massimo. He shuffled the cards, dealt them three each and four face up on the table. The first game of Scopa began.

What began as a sop to please his parents turned into a couple of hours' mindless fun under the warm starry sky. His parents were the most laid-back, easy-going people on the planet but when it came to card games, they became ultra-competitive.

And Livia's competitive streak came out too. His wife and mother were both determined to beat their spouses and were not above cheating to achieve this. When the women were two nil down, suddenly they both found it necessary to halt the game for frequent bathroom breaks.

Soon after this mysterious onset of bladder issues, he spotted his mother furtively pulling something out of her handbag, which, when she was challenged, turned out to be a king with a value of ten points. Rather than display any shame, his mother giggled. Livia though… her throaty cackle of laughter filled his ears and suddenly he was thrown back to his sister's wedding and the first time he'd heard it.

It was a sound that speared him.

Firmly dragging his mind away from that fateful first meeting, he confiscated the card but then found he couldn't stop his own burst of laughter when, barely a minute later, Livia stood to use the bathroom for the fourth time and two high-value cards slipped out of her top.

'Shameless,' he chided with a stern shake of his head.

'All's fair in love and war,' she replied, a gleam in her eye he hadn't seen for so long that suddenly he could fight the swelling emotions no more, body blows of longing and pain ravaging him.

He couldn't tear his gaze from her.

In the beat of a moment her amusement vanished and her dark brown eyes were swirling with more emotion than there were stars in the sky.

Hardly single-digit seconds passed as their stares remained fixed on each other but those seconds contained so much weight he felt its compression on his chest. He knew with a bone-deep certainty that she was thinking about their first meeting too and that the memory lanced her as deeply as it did him.

Then Livia turned her gaze from him.

'I really do need to use the bathroom,' she murmured, reaching down to pick up the illicit cards and placing them on the table.

In the plush ladies' room, Livia put her hands on the sink and dragged air into her lungs.

For a moment there her heart had felt so full of so many emotions that it had felt as if it could burst out of her chest.

Teaming up with Sera against their husbands had been so wickedly joyful that for a while she had forgotten that she and Massimo were estranged and preparing for a divorce.

For a short, glorious time, it had been like slipping on a pair of shoes that transported them to their early days when there had been as much fun in their marriage as there had been desire and love.

She had adored making Massimo laugh. He was such a serious person that to see his face light up had brought her more joy than anything. Laughter had been in short supply in her childhood so to discover this side of herself with him had been joyful in its own right.

Like the smiles she'd been unable to form in the four months since she'd left him, laughter had become a distant memory too. Until tonight.

Back outside in the warm evening air, she found the cards had been put away and the glasses empty. Sera and Gianni got to their feet as she approached the table and both apologised for having to call it a night. They were tired and needed to get some sleep.

Kissing them both goodnight, Livia poured

herself another bourbon and watched them walk away.

The silence they left behind was stark. Apart from the white noise in her ears.

'I suppose we should go to our chalet too,' she said, avoiding Massimo's stare.

They'd spent a whole day travelling between time zones quickly followed by a day out at sea. All of this, when added to her frazzled nerves brought about by being with him again, was a recipe for exhaustion. Yet she felt anything but tired.

When he didn't answer, she stared up at the sky. The stars were in abundance that night, twinkling like gold diamonds in the vast blackness. She'd thought the sky in LA was big but here, on this island, it seemed to stretch for ever.

'I'll sleep on the sofa,' she added into the silence.

'No. You take the bed.' She felt his eyes on her. 'I've work I need to get on with.'

'The sofa's too small for you, and you can't work all night.' But he could. She knew that.

He'd worked through the night on many occasions.

'I'll work for a few hours then sleep on the hammock.'

'We have a hammock?' That was the first she'd heard of it.

'I'm surprised you didn't notice it earlier. It's on the veranda by the outside table.'

'I probably didn't register it,' she murmured, taking a hasty sip of her bourbon.

She wouldn't have noticed any hammock because when she'd stepped out onto the veranda her eyes had been too consumed by Massimo to register anything else.

They finished their drinks and, as silently as they'd made the walk from their chalet to the lodge, walked the return journey together. The incoming tide now lapped the beach noisily, so deep beneath the bridge that if this had been her first sight of the island she would never have believed it could ebb back far enough for a sandy pathway to open up between the main island and their private peninsula.

But as much as she tried to distract herself

with their surroundings she couldn't block out Massimo's lean frame striding beside her.

When they reached their chalet, he picked up the briefcase he'd left on their dining table.

Everything about this chalet was supposed to be theirs. Everything had been designed to their exact instructions; a love nest they'd imagined themselves escaping to whenever time allowed, designed and dreamed up before Livia had realised time would never allow it. For Massimo, time existed only for work.

He stared at her for a moment before his chest rose sharply. 'I'll work on the veranda. Sleep well.'

Her goodnight to him came out as a whisper.

He closed the door quietly behind him.

Massimo powered his laptop but, other than reply to a few urgent emails, found he didn't have the concentration to work.

Sighing heavily, he ran his fingers through his hair and closed his eyes.

It felt as if he'd slipped into a time loop, taken back to the days when he'd worked from the sprawling building that homed Briatore

Technologies and found his concentration fighting a war with himself. Livia had taken back possession of his mind. She'd been all he could think of then. She was all he could think of now.

It didn't matter, he told himself grimly. One more full day and night and then that would be it for them. She would live her life in Italy and he would live his in LA.

Thinking he could do with another drink before attempting to sleep in the hammock he'd instructed be erected when he'd remembered the chalet he would share with his estranged wife had only one bed, he padded quietly back inside. Before he could switch the light on and head to the bar, he noticed a slant of light coming from beneath the closed bedroom door.

His heart fisted.

He'd left her over an hour ago, plenty of time for her to do her night-time beauty routine and fall asleep. Was she reading?

Was she wearing the cream pyjamas that managed to be both modest and yet revealing...?

He stepped closer to the bedroom door, his

ears craning when he heard her voice. She was talking to someone.

A lover?

Hating himself yet unable to stop, he put his ear to the door. The wooden barrier muffled her words.

She laughed. It sounded pained. And then she said something distinguishable even through the muffling.

'Please. I love you.'

CHAPTER SEVEN

NIGHTMARES HAD PLAGUED Livia's life as far back as she could remember but it was rare for them to pepper her sleep over a whole night. After a night of exactly that and feeling distinctly unrefreshed, she showered and dressed quickly, choosing a black bikini, mid-thigh-length denim shorts and a loose white top.

Years of practice had allowed her to switch her mind off from her brother's problems—she would never have slept a wink if she hadn't—but last night his problems had been too great to stop her from worrying.

She had a feeling that even without Gianluca's issues overshadowing everything, she would still have had problems sleeping. She had never successfully learned to switch her mind off from her husband.

Their bed had been everything they'd been

promised, like sleeping on a supportive cloud. Having never shared it with Massimo, she'd assumed she'd be all right sleeping in it alone but her twitchy body had betrayed her. This was a bed designed for lovers, chosen when divorce hadn't entered her head.

Before leaving the chalet she checked her phone, hoping Gianluca had messaged as he'd promised he would. Her chest loosened a fraction to see his simple message on the screen telling her he was fine and that nothing had happened.

The message did nothing to quell the sick dread curdling in her stomach.

Out on the veranda she wasn't surprised to find Massimo awake, dressed in the same clothes he'd worn the previous evening, and drinking a cup of coffee at the table. He must have made it while she'd been showering.

He would have heard the shower. He would have known she was awake. He hadn't thought to make her a coffee too.

It hurt that he hadn't thought of her, especially since she'd made him a coffee barely twelve hours ago. It had been an attempt at a peace offering she'd assumed—wrongly—that he'd accepted.

Her attention was caught by the hammock behind him swinging between the low roof of the chalet and one of the palm trees.

How had she not noticed it before?

Pushing petty thoughts of coffee aside, she inclined her head towards the hammock. 'How did you find sleeping on that?'

He shrugged in answer.

'I don't mind sleeping on it tonight.'

'No need,' he answered sardonically. 'It was fine.'

'But it doesn't seem fair...'

'I said no need,' he said through what sounded like gritted teeth before rising to his feet. 'I'm going to take a shower.'

Her eyes narrowed. Since when did Massimo wake up in such an obviously foul mood? She had a strong inkling his ire was directed at her, although she couldn't think what she'd done to cause it. 'Suit yourself. I'm going to make a coffee. I would offer you one but seeing as you've already taken care of yourself, I won't bother.'

His smile was as cutting as his tone had been. 'Good.'

Despite her much shorter legs, Livia made it to the chalet ahead of him.

Inside, he strode past her and into the bedroom, closing the door firmly behind him.

She scowled at the door and wished she had laser eyes that could cut through it and zap him.

She hoped he regretted suggesting the main bathroom be adjacent to where they slept.

In the small yet eye-wateringly expensive kitchen area, she opened a cupboard door, removed a glass mug then closed it with a slam. One small spoonful of sugar was thrown into the mug before she snatched an espresso pod and rammed it into the machine, then punched the button to get it working.

Alone in the bathroom, Massimo looked at the beauty paraphernalia left higgledy-piggledy all over the ledge and rammed his hands into his pockets to prevent them sweeping the entire lot onto the floor.

From the sounds of banging coming from the kitchen area, Livia was having more trouble controlling her own temper. But then, she always had.

His fury, he recognised in a dim, grim fashion, should be aimed at himself.

Until he'd heard her utter words of love to another, he'd never believed in his heart that she'd found someone else. The confirmation that she had a lover had come as a bigger blow than he'd ever imagined it could.

Seeing her in the flesh for the first time since hearing that confirmation had lanced him; a different pain from the constant ache he'd learned to live with since she'd left him. This pain went far deeper.

How could he go on pretending all was well in their marriage knowing another man had kissed those lips, knowing her pretty hands had touched another's body?

Was it for her lover that she'd cut her hair and added colour to it?

Nausea roiled deep in his stomach and he stripped his clothes off and threw them onto the floor, kicking his jeans for good measure.

Knowing that volatile emotions were usually his wife's domain only increased his temper.

Setting the temperature to cold, he stood under the frigid water for as long as he could bear it. It did little to temper the violent emotions churning in him.

After donning shorts and a T-shirt in his private dressing room—at least he was spared having to dress surrounded by Livia's clothing—he stepped back into the bedroom and this time was unable to stop his eyes falling to the neatly made bed.

It was a habit he'd never been able to break her out of. In LA she'd insisted on making it herself even though his housekeeping team would go into their bedroom later on and remake it to hotel standards.

The tightness in his lungs loosened a little.

He shouldn't take his unfathomable jealousy out on Livia. She had done nothing wrong. Their marriage was over.

But his calm rationale flew out of the window when he went back into the main living area and found her slumped on the sofa, her feet on the coffee table, ankles hooked together, fingers flying on the screen of her phone, concentration etched on her face. An empty glass mug lay on a coaster only inches from her bare feet.

More contact with her lover? he wondered bleakly.

She didn't look at him but a mutinous expression he recognised formed on her face. 'Are you going to tell me what I've done to upset you?'

'You haven't done anything,' he answered stiffly.

She made a pft sound he recognised. It had become a familiar sound in the months leading up to her leaving him.

'I didn't sleep well,' he confessed, attempting a less hostile tone.

'You said you'd been fine on the hammock.'

'It wasn't the hammock. I couldn't switch my mind off.' This much was the truth. How could he sleep when his mind tortured him with images of his wife with another man?

Now her eyes did rise to meet his. He saw suspicion in the dark brown depths. After long moments, she sighed and put her phone down on the coffee table. 'Okay,' she said with a shrug.

Massimo was an insomniac, Livia reminded herself. Switching his mind off enough to sleep was a battle he'd fought his entire life.

But never, not even when they'd been in the midst of their cold war, had he woken in such an obviously foul temper. She didn't believe for a minute that it was lack of sleep causing his current mood but experience had taught her the futility of trying to get him to open up.

Her phone vibrated and bounced on the table. Snatching it up, she read the message that had pinged in and sighed again.

'Problem?' Massimo asked.

Even though she could feel the animosity in his politely delivered question and even though his bad mood had perversely put her in a bad mood too, the growing panic in her belly needed an outlet.

She rubbed her eyes with the palms of her hands and looked back at him. 'Gianluca.'

A furrow grooved in his brow. 'What's happened?'

'Don Fortunato's requested a meeting with him.' She didn't need to tell him what that meant. She had spared him nothing about the world she'd grown up in. The meeting could only mean one thing—that Gianluca would be invited to 'prove' himself. If he proved himself successfully then he would become one of Don Fortunato's trusted foot soldiers, a marked step up from his current role as a watcher.

The groove deepened. 'Requested? So he hasn't met with him yet?'

'Not yet, no. He's been summoned to his home this evening.' If Gianluca wanted the life Don Fortunato was offering, this would be a summons he'd been hoping for. Their father's loyalty and death had marked all the Esposito children as foot soldiers of the future. Now it was Gianluca's turn to prove himself a man.

'What's he going to do?'

'I don't know.' She pinched the bridge of her nose and tried to calm her rabid thoughts. Pasquale had been summoned for this same meeting within days of his sixteenth birthday. Livia had lost him that night. Gianluca's immaturity must have been noted for he'd been given an extra two years before his summons. It felt as if she'd spent these two years doing nothing but beg him to take the lifeline she was offering and escape.

If he went ahead and met Don Fortunato tonight, there would be no escape. Whatever he was tasked to do would be much more than dipping a toe in their criminal world.

'I've offered him money and I've already got a room set up for him at my apartment. He wants to leave but he's scared.' And she was scared too; far more frightened for her baby brother than she had ever been for herself.

'When did he tell you this?'

'Last night. He called when I was in bed.'

'Last night?' he clarified. There was an expression on his face, a flickering she couldn't interpret.

She nodded heavily. 'He's always known this day would come but inside he always thought it would be tomorrow. He's been happy roving around with his friends on their stupid scooters and chasing girls... How cruel is fate that the day it comes I'm on the other side of the world and unable to help him?'

All the plans she'd made to help him flee were worthless. She was too far away. Gianluca was technically an adult but emotionally he was still a child. She didn't know if he had the strength to break away without her own strength to encourage and sustain him.

She watched Massimo stride to the kitchen area and pull two glass mugs out of the cupboard.

'How did you escape, Livia?' he asked thoughtfully, placing both mugs in the coffee machine.

'You know how. I took my money and jumped on a train and never looked back.'

He put a large pod in the machine and pressed the button. 'You did that without help?'

'You know I did but I wasn't in his position.'

'Has Gianluca saved any money?'

'No.' Saving was an alien concept to her brother. 'I've offered to transfer him the money for his ticket out but he's scared to take it. He knows they're watching him.'

Frustration burned deeply enough for her to want to scream. Gianluca looked up to her. If she were in Italy she would be right there, her hand extended, a source of strength and a physical reminder that it was possible to leave and possible to build a good life outside the Secondigliano.

'Are you sure he wants to leave?'

'*Yes.* The summons has frightened him.' She managed a twisted smile then twisted her fingers together to stop herself biting the horrible gel stuff off her nails. 'I think my baby brother has grown up overnight.'

He stirred their coffees and carried them over, handing one to her.

Strangely, the hostility that had been shooting off him had gone.

He sat opposite her. 'Let me speak to him.'

'You? What for?'

'I can help.'

'How? You're as far away from him as I am.'

'But I have resources at my disposal that you don't. Have you heard of Felipe Lorenzi?'

She shook her head.

'He's ex-Spanish Special Forces and now runs his own security business protecting high-profile people. He only employs other ex-special forces. They're the best at what they do and used to dangerous situations. They can get him out safely.'

She stared at him dumbly. She'd confided in Massimo only because her fears for her brother had grown so large she'd felt as if she would explode if she kept them contained a minute longer. She hadn't expected him to offer help. It hadn't crossed her mind.

'You would do that?' she whispered. She hardly dared allow hope to fight through the fear. If they could get Gianluca out before his meeting with Don Fortunato, before he was tasked with something that would cross the line for ever and before he was made privy to the secrets that would put a mark on his head, then there was a good chance he would be left in peace.

He reached into his pocket and pulled out his phone. 'Leave it with me. By the time of my grandfather's party tonight, your brother will be out of the Secondigliano and free.'

Having Livia's brother to concentrate on and the preparations for the party that evening to oversee helped the day pass quickly. It kept Massimo's mind occupied. It stopped him having to think of the relief that had almost doubled him over to learn his wife hadn't been exchanging endearments with a lover.

She'd been talking to her brother.

But this only caused a shadow to form on his relief because he knew he had no right feeling relief. He had no business feeling what he'd felt.

Knowing how he should feel and behave did nothing to stop the twisting ache that had burrowed in his guts and set up home in his short time on the island. He had to get a grip on it. One day in the future Livia would find a new lover who could give her the happiness she deserved, a man who could give her the attention and time she needed.

He couldn't imagine meeting anyone for himself. A casual lover, possibly, if his body ever became receptive to a woman who wasn't his wife. He would certainly never marry again. Or have children. Before he'd met Livia he'd never even thought of having children. The subject had completely passed by his radar.

Her pointed remark that theirs had been no marriage to bring a child into had hit a nerve with its truth. He would be as lousy a father as he'd been a husband.

Before he could switch his mind away from his latest bout of acidic ruminations and call his PA for a business update, he spotted two figures approaching in the distance. Livia was returning from her walk with his grandfather. They'd gone for an exploration of the island that had been his grandfather's home together. She was the only member of the family Massimo felt comfortable for his grandfather to spend time alone with. If there was an emergency she would know exactly what to do.

Whatever his conflicting feelings towards his estranged wife, he would never deny that she was an exceptional nurse who'd cared for his grandfather with a devotion that had allowed the entire family to sleep at night. Her return to nursing would be other cancer sufferers' gain.

He failed to stop his heart blooming as she neared him. His blood stirred too, thickening the closer she came. She'd removed her T-shirt and tied it around her waist, exposing her bikini-clad breasts, which swayed gently as she walked towards him pushing the wheel-chair. Her hair, normally worn loose, had been pulled into a high ponytail, no doubt to counter the heat coming from the blazing sun. Her golden skin had darkened in their short time on the island and it suited her beautifully.

His grandfather had fallen asleep. She adjusted the parasol above him then gave Massimo a cautious smile. 'Any news?'

He looked at his watch. 'One hour.'

Felipe's wife, Francesca, was about to go into labour with their second child so his right-hand man, Seb, was coordinating events. Seb had been confident they could get Gianluca out without anyone noticing their presence. But this depended on Gianluca following the plan and being in the right place at the right time without changing his mind.

If Gianluca had half the strength of mind his sister had, then everything would go well.

If was a big word and Massimo had his doubts. He hoped for Livia's sake that Gianluca went through with it. He didn't like to think of her devastation if the opposite happened.

She would cope though. That was one thing

he didn't doubt. Livia was a tough cookie. The life she'd lived, the life they were now trying to remove her brother from, had made her that way.

This was the first time since he'd met her, though, that the reality of her childhood had seeped into their life together. Her childhood had always been stories narrated from the safety and comfort of their bed, fables completely removed from his own existence. He'd appreciated intellectually what an awful life it had been for her but this was the first time he'd really *felt* it. It was as if her fear had transplanted like ice in his heart.

'As soon as I have word, I will let you know,' he promised. Gianluca had been instructed to turn his phone off in case it had a tracker in it. Massimo had already organised a replacement one for him.

'Thank you.' Her lips pulled together before her chest and shoulders rose then fell sharply. 'Whatever happens...thank you.'

His own chest inflated at this simple, sincere gratitude. He hadn't offered assistance out of any form of altruism. Livia had needed help and he'd been in a position to provide it...

He'd never seen fear on her face before. He defied any man in his position not to offer their help too.

It struck him then that in the whole of their marriage she had never asked for or needed his help for anything of importance. Not once. All she'd ever wanted from him was the one thing he'd been unable to give. His time.

Her shoulders rose again. 'I'm going to find one of Jimmy's carers and get them to put him to bed, then I'll be back out to help...if you want it?'

As she spoke, a golf buggy delivering the first batch of workers for the evening's party emerged from the thick forest. There was much to oversee to ensure the event went perfectly. His family had offered help earlier but he'd refused, told them to enjoy their last full day on the island. This was something he'd wanted to do himself. His last gift to his grandfather.

About to give the same refusal to Livia, he found his tongue forming words of its own accord. 'If you haven't anything better to do.'

Her smile this time was wide. 'Only sun-bathing, which bores me.'

She wheeled his grandfather away.

He closed his eyes and breathed deeply, telling himself he'd accepted her offer so as to give her something to distract herself with while they waited for news on her brother.

The acid burning in his guts exposed that for the lie it was.

Livia, her head upside down, dried her hair on a low setting and tried to pretend she wasn't keeping an ear out for Massimo. He'd sent her back to their chalet over an hour ago saying he'd join her shortly. The party was due to start in thirty minutes and he still needed to shower and dress. This was cutting it fine even for the man who could get himself ready in ten minutes flat.

Together, they'd supervised the arrival of the vast volume of staff employed for the evening, the exquisite finger buffet the army of chefs had spent the day preparing, the decoration of the interior and exterior of the lodge, the quantities and varieties of drink, made sure the extra chalets some of the guests were staying in for the night were ready, and fielded a constant flow of calls.

During all this, Massimo had kept her updated on Gianluca. As of three hours ago her brother was in a hotel two hundred miles from Naples. Tomorrow he'd be moved from the hotel to her rented apartment.

Knowing her brother was safe and had turned his back on the life she too had fought so hard to escape from had left her dizzy with relief. Every part of her felt the relief, her lungs looser, her limbs stronger, her shoulders lighter. She could hardly wait to get back to Rome and smother him.

Massimo's help in extracting Gianluca...

She'd learned at much too young an age that to get through life she could only rely on herself. Self-reliance had been so inured in her that it had never occurred to her to ask for help. She'd always managed alone.

It was the first time anyone had ever removed a burden from her shoulders and her heart swelled in gratitude for it.

Maybe Gianluca would have found the nerve

to leave on his own that day with nothing but a transfer of money from her and the promise of her apartment but there was no doubt that Massimo taking control of the situation had given Gianluca the final injection of courage he needed. *He'd* been the one to talk Gianluca round.

When Gianluca had called her from the hotel, he'd been relieved to be out but torn at all he was leaving behind. She understood those feelings. They were the same emotions she'd lived through. As dangerous an environment as the Secondigliano was, it was where their family and friends were. It was their home. Starting over was never easy.

Leaving Massimo had been harder than leaving her family. She'd never felt an atom of relief at leaving him, only overwhelming pain. The future without him had never appeared bright, only bleak.

There had been times that day when she'd found herself staring at him with a heart so full she'd felt the individual heavy beats vibrating through her body.

There had been times, too, when she'd had

to turn her face away from him and blink back hot tears at all they had lost. Today, working together harmoniously, supporting each other, teasing each other, laughing…it was like being thrown back to the early days of their marriage.

Why had they thrown it away?

When she'd finished drying her hair, she heard yet another small plane flying low over the cabin. More guests arriving. Unfortunately—or fortunately, depending on your perspective of paradise being spoilt by a mile-long runway—the island only had the capacity to admit small aircraft, so half the guests were being flown in as the staff had been: tag-team-style. The remaining guests were sailing to the island on Massimo's yacht.

She'd just finished applying her lipstick when the bedroom door opened and Massimo's reflection appeared in the mirror.

She stared at him, her chest filling so hard and so quickly that it pushed the air from her lungs.

She cleared her throat and turned around to face him properly, trying desperately hard to mask the turbulence raging beneath her skin. 'I was about to send a search party out for you.'

Caramel eyes glittered. His throat moved a number of times before he responded with a gruff, 'I had a work call I needed to take care of. Give me ten minutes?'

She nodded.

He strode to the bathroom door and turned the handle.

As he pushed it open, he suddenly stopped and turned back to face her. His throat moved again. 'You look beautiful.'

CHAPTER EIGHT

THE SETTING SUN bathed the lodge in a warm golden glow. The glow bounced off the delicate lights that adorned the exterior of the lodge and the high trees nestled around it, creating a sight that made Livia sigh with pleasure. The abundance of flowering shrubs filled the air with exotic scents that seemed more pronounced than usual to her sensitised state.

The lodge's huge double doors were open. Music and chattering voices echoed out of it like a friendly greeting.

She walked in step with Massimo, heartbreakingly gorgeous in a black tuxedo and a black tie she doubted would stay around his neck for any length of time. In thirteen minutes flat he'd showered, dressed and trimmed his beard. He'd even tamed his thick black hair.

From the moment they'd closed their chalet

door behind them, the urge to take his hand had been all-consuming. It swung by his hip as he made his graceful long strides. All she had to do was stretch her fingers...

Temptation was taken away when they entered the lodge. They were welcomed by a sea of happy faces all dressed in their finest clothes, embraces and smacking kisses flowing free and fast.

Madeline pounced at the earliest opportunity. 'Come with me and introduce yourself to anyone you've never met before,' she hissed in Livia's ear. 'Everyone seems to know my name but I have no idea who lots of them are and I don't want to embarrass myself or them by saying so.'

Laughing, Livia happily stepped into the throng and introduced herself to the strangers, making sure to repeat their names for Madeline's benefit. A handful were Jimmy's old childhood friends, people who had once called this island home, others soldiers he'd befriended during his voluntary deployment in the Second World War. In all, there were ninety guests celebrating Jimmy's birthday with him. The language barrier between herself and the native English speakers was easy to overcome, she found, by simply placing her hand to her chest and reciting her name. After that, Madeline would take over and translate.

Getting everyone to the island for the party had been a logistical nightmare but the look on Jimmy's face proved all the effort Massimo had made and the vast expense had been worth it. Currently talking to an old school-friend who was in his own wheelchair and had his own carer in attendance, Jimmy was smiling from ear to ear.

Livia's heart swelled with love for the elderly man whose home she had entered as his nurse and left as his granddaughter-in-law. He had an inherent kindness and a decency about him that had shone through from their first meeting, qualities inherent in his daughter and granddaughter too. This was the kind of family Livia had longed for as a child. A family where you felt safe and cocooned in love. There had been love of a sort in the Esposito home but it was a hard love, the kind that came with conditions.

Her gaze drifted to Jimmy's grandson and somehow her heart swelled even more. Massimo was on his haunches chatting to a frail great-aunt. Massimo was different from the rest of his family in more ways than she could count but he had their decency. He had an unlimited quota of generosity running through his veins. All this, the purchase of the island, the building of the entire complex…all of that had been achieved by Massimo so Jimmy could spend his final birthday in the place of his birth.

The island would also be Jimmy's legacy. The staff employed to work full-time on the resort doubled as wardens for the nature reserve. Jimmy's offspring and his siblings' offspring would enjoy this paradise for generations to come. All of it courtesy of Massimo.

Massimo tried to concentrate on what his great-aunt, a woman he'd never met before, was saying to him. Her heavily accented English flew like a burr from her mouth. Her gratitude towards Massimo for arranging the party and ensuring she got to see her youngest brother for the first time in almost seventy years touched him. He imagined her as a young girl playing with his grandfather and their other siblings, the last generation of Seibuas to live, work and play here before their way of life had become unsustainable.

But it wasn't her accent that made it hard for him to concentrate. His lack of concentration was down to his wife.

She always looked beautiful but tonight… Beauty did not do her justice. He had to fight his eyes' desire to keep seeking her out but somehow he was always fully aware of exactly where she was. Right then, she was at the buffet table with his father.

The mid-thigh-length strappy black sequined dress she wore with its plunging neckline, the gold locket she wore around her neck, the gold hooped earrings that gleamed through the locks of her hair…

Everything about her glittered.

The Livia he'd first met had come back to life. The confident, gregarious woman with the throaty, dirty laugh, the woman who'd never found language to be a barrier for communication, she was here, radiating with the joy of life.

And why shouldn't she radiate in it? Life for Livia had been a hard-fought battle.

Where had this woman gone in those awful cold months before she'd left him?

He knew her brother's escape had something to do with her carefree mood but there had to be a greater explanation than that.

Suddenly her stance shifted and her eyes fell on him.

That feeling of being punch-drunk hit him again.

He had no idea how long they stared at each other. He barely recalled his last few minutes of conversation with his great-aunt either.

In need of a drink, he was manoeuvring his way around small children dancing vigorously, when his grandfather caught his eye and beckoned him over.

Massimo squatted to the same level as his wheelchair and took his frail hands into his own. It was like touching tissue paper. 'Are you enjoying the party, *Nonno*?'

'You have made an old man very happy. Thank you.'

Massimo would never get used to the raspiness of his grandfather's voice. He squeezed the frail hands gently. 'My pleasure.'

The filmy eyes that had once been the same colour as Massimo's held his and the old gleam in them returned. 'What does an old man have to do to get a bourbon here?'

'I thought you'd been advised against drinking alcohol?'

'What does advice matter when you're dying?'

Massimo winced.

His grandfather twisted his hands so he was the one holding Massimo's. He leaned closer to him. 'I'm not afraid of death, Massimo. I've had a good life. All the people here remind me how good it's been. I've *lived*, and the short time I have left, I want to live that too.'

There was no guile in his grandfather's stare but Massimo had the strong impression the elderly man was trying to tell him something.

He kissed the bald head and wished he knew the words to tell his grandfather how much he meant to him.

By the time he returned with his grandfather's drink, a crowd had gathered around him. Not wanting to be snared in a large group and forced to make more small talk, he decided an upgrade from the beer he'd been drinking was in order and went back to the bar to order himself a large bourbon.

He was on his second when Livia sidled up to him.

'Hiding away?' she asked.

'Taking a breather.'

Dark brown eyes studied him, a combination of sympathy and amusement in them. Livia knew well how social situations made him feel.

She caught the barman's attention and ordered herself a bourbon too. 'This is a great party.'

'People are enjoying it?'

'Very much.' She nudged him with her elbow and pointed at one of the sofas. Two of the small children he'd almost tripped over earlier were fast asleep on it. A third, who'd gone a pale green colour, was eating a large scoop of ice cream, utter determination etched on her face. 'Someone needs to get that girl a sick bag.'

He laughed and was immediately thrown back to his sister's wedding again.

He'd approached Livia at the bar. She'd said something inane that had made him laugh. He wished he could remember what it was but it had slipped away the moment she'd said it, his attention too transfixed on her for words to stick.

She'd blown him away.

Those same feelings…

Had they ever really left him?

The music had slowed in tempo. The dance floor had filled, the children making way for the adults.

'We should dance,' he murmured.

Her chest rose, head tilted, teeth grazing over her bottom lip. 'I suppose we should… for appearances' sake.'

He breathed deeply and slowly held his hand out.

Equally slowly, she stretched hers out to meet his. The pads of her fingers pressed into his palm. Tingles shot through his skin. His fingers closed over them.

On the crowded dance floor, he placed his hands loosely on her hips. Her hands rested lightly on his shoulders. A delicate waft of her perfume filtered through his airwaves.

He clenched his jaw and purposely kept his gaze focused above her head.

They moved slowly in tempo with the music, their bodies a whisper away from touching…

'When did you take your tie off?' Livia murmured when she couldn't take the tension that had sprung between them any longer.

She'd been trying very hard not to breathe. Every inhalation sent Massimo's familiar musky heat and the citrus undertones of his cologne darting into her airwaves. Her skin vibrated with awareness, her senses uncoiling, tiny springs straining towards the man whose hands hardly touched her hips. She could feel the weight in them though, piercing through her skin.

Caramel eyes slowly drifted down to meet her gaze.

The music beating around them reduced to a burr.

The breath of space between them closed. The tips of her breasts brushed against the top of his flat stomach. The weight of his hands increased in pressure.

Heat pulsed deep in her pelvis.

Her hands crept without conscious thought over his shoulder blades. Heart beating hard, her fingers found his neck…her palms pressed against it.

His right hand caressed slowly up her back. She shivered at the darts of sensation rippling through her.

Distantly, she was aware the song they were dancing to had finished.

His left hand drew across her lower back and gradually pulled her so close their bodies became flush.

Her cheek pressed into his shoulder. She could feel the heavy thuds of his heart. They matched the beats of hers.

His mouth pressed into the top of her head. The warmth of his ragged breath whispered in the strands of her hair. Her lungs had stopped functioning. Not a hitch of air went into them.

A finger brushed a lock of her hair.

She closed her eyes.

The lock was caught and wound in his fingers.

She turned her cheek and pressed her mouth to his throat…

A body slammed into them. Words, foreign to her drumming ears but unmistakably words of apology, were gabbled.

They pulled apart.

There was a flash of bewilderment in Massimo's eyes she knew must be mirrored in hers before he blinked it away.

A song famous at parties all around the world was now playing. The floor was packed with bodies all joining in with the accompanying dance. Even the passed-out children had woken up to join in with it.

And she'd been oblivious. They both had.

The rest of the party passed in a blur, as if she'd been sucked into a time warp that had her in Massimo's arms on the crowded dance floor one minute, the next following him into their chalet. Had they even spoken since they'd left the dance floor?

Vague images flashed in Livia's mind. Jimmy, ably assisted by all the children under the age of ten blowing out the ninety candles on his cake. The exchange of goodbye kisses.

After the noise of the party, the silence in their chalet was deafening.

She stared at Massimo with a thundering heart and tried to think of something, anything to say to cut through this tension-filled silence but her brain seemed to have been infected with a fever.

His chest rose before he nodded his head in a decisive manner. 'I'll brush my teeth and leave you to sleep.'

Every inch of her body screamed in protest.

She managed to incline her head.

He turned and disappeared into the bedroom.

Massimo brushed his teeth vigorously, as if the bristles could brush away the longing raging through him.

One dance with Livia had smashed through his defences.

One touch of her hand had set his pulses racing.

One look in her eyes had set his heart pounding.

One press of her body against his had set the arousal he'd been suppressing by a thread off in an unstoppable flow that denial had no longer been able to contain.

He could still feel her lips against his throat. That one brush had marked him. His body still buzzed from the thrills that had been unleashed in that one short dance.

He wanted her with an ache that burned. He'd never *stopped* wanting her.

Done with his teeth, he slapped cold water over his face then stared hard at his reflection.

He was going to leave this bathroom, walk calmly through the bedroom, wish Livia a good night then go outside and sleep on the hammock.

He would not linger. He would not engage in conversation. He would not touch her.

To do any of these things would prise open

the lid of the box they had both hammered shut. Their marriage was over for damn good reasons. In the morning they would say goodbye and fly to separate continents. The ripping of his heart at this thought meant nothing but an acknowledgement of his own failure. For a man who had succeeded on his own merits at everything he'd attempted in life, failure was a hard thing to tolerate. Their marriage had been a failure and much of that had been down to him. It was bound to sit uncomfortably.

He patted his damp face dry, shoved the towel back on the rail and moved purposefully out of the bathroom, through the bedroom that had been designed to be theirs, and through to the main living area…

Livia was in the kitchen area, her back to the counter, glass of water clasped tightly in her hand.

Their eyes met.

His heart squeezed unbearably but his steps did not falter.

'Sleep well,' he muttered as he continued to the door.

Only when he'd closed the door behind him did he pause for breath.

He closed his eyes and filled his lungs with resolve…

But he could still feel her eyes on him.

He fisted a hand and punched it into the palm of the other.

He tried to set off again. His legs and feet refused to cooperate.

Livia stared at the closed door for so long her eyes became fuzzy.

There was a cramping in her chest that made every breath she took an effort.

She wanted to run out after him and beg him to come back inside. She wanted to wrap her arms around him and kiss him; his mouth, his face, his neck, his chest, every inch of him.

She wanted his arms around her. She wanted to feel the intense pleasure that had cemented the love they had once found together.

Deep in her soul she knew she would never find what they'd had with anyone else. It wasn't possible for a heart to love as deeply as hers had loved Massimo and move on without leaving a part of it with him.

And he had loved her too. He *had*. Self-preservation had had her denying his love but being with him again had unleashed the memories she'd suppressed about all the good times they'd had.

Those good times had been the best of her life.

She'd *had* to focus on the bad times that had destroyed them because to remember the good times would have been to remind herself in multicolour detail of all they had thrown away.

Resolve suddenly took her in its grip, pulling her out of the paralysis that had kept her immobile in her desperate thoughts.

Shoving her undrunk glass of water on the counter, she kicked her shoes off and put one bare foot in front of the other…

Without any warning the door flew open.

Massimo filled the doorway, breathing heavily through his nose, his hair dishevelled, caramel eyes pulsing.

There was a moment of stillness. Only a moment but it stretched and pulled like an invisible band looping around them, pulling tighter and tighter until the binds became too great and, feet moving in sync, they closed the distance between them.

Livia drank in the face she had never stopped dreaming about. Everything inside her had cramped. Except for her heart. That felt as if a hummingbird had nestled in it.

The throat she had unthinkingly kissed moved. The top three buttons of his shirt were undone. The dinner jacket he'd worn to the party had long been discarded with the tie that had adorned his neck.

This was Massimo; heartbreakingly handsome yet unkempt, lacking in vanity and dismissive of his own beauty. Yet he had made her feel feminine and beautiful. He had made her feel as if she were the only woman on this earth.

The look reflecting back at her now...

It made all those old feelings come roaring back to life.

The electrified air between them swirled as his hand inched to hers. Fingers locked together. Slowly, he lifted their hands to his chest as, equally slowly, his other hand touched her hair. Using the backs of his fingers, he stroked the strands.

How could hair feel alive? she wondered dimly, shivering as sensation tingled from the top of her head and spread through her heated veins.

Their entwined fingers tightened.

The hand in her hair dived through the locks and gently traced the rim of her ear.

Her legs weakened.

The hand at her ear slowly skimmed down the side of her neck. The hummingbird in her heart was trying to beat its way out. It almost succeeded when the eyes her gaze was locked on drew closer and closer, the lids closing, and the wide, firm mouth she had once believed she would kiss for ever brushed against her aching lips.

CHAPTER NINE

MASSIMO, EYES CLOSED, rested his mouth against the softest lips in creation and breathed Livia in.

He felt her quiver. The nails of the fingers entwined in his dug into his hand.

Emotions were erupting through him, so many it was impossible to pinpoint one and say *this* was what he was feeling.

The only certainty he could find was that this was where he needed to be.

He needed Livia's touch like a fish needed water.

And he needed to touch her like a drowning man needed air.

A tempest raged inside him, a storm crashing onto the drowning man.

Livia was the air he needed. She was on his mind with every breath he took.

The thunder of his heart vibrated through his bones. When she placed her small hand on the top of his chest he knew she must be able to feel it too.

He could feel her heartbeat through their tightly wound hands.

The fingers splayed on her soft neck drifted back up to spear her hair. He hadn't realised that he'd been afraid the changes she'd made to her hair would have changed its texture until relief had coursed through him on the dance floor to find it had the same silky feel.

He'd been as helpless not to touch her then as he was not to touch her now.

Livia was more than air. She was the fire in his heart, the water in his veins, the earth that kept him grounded.

Their lips moved slowly together, fused mouths parting, the kiss deepening.

Her sweet breath curled into his senses.

Their entwined hands released. Arms wrapped tightly around each other, bodies crushed together, tongues danced as the desire he had fought since she had stepped into the cabin of his private jet was finally set free.

A million tastes and scents and sensations filled Livia's starved senses. Being wrapped so tightly in Massimo's arms and being kissed so deeply and passionately was awakening the last parts of her she had kept locked away.

He'd torn the last of her barriers down but the feelings erupting in her were too heady, too familiar and too wondrous to be frightening.

If she were to be cast away on a desert island and allowed to choose only one person to join her on it, there was no question of who she would choose. Massimo. He was scarred on her heart and etched in her soul.

She didn't want to think of what she was doing—what they were doing. She needed this too much. Needed him too much.

Only now, as she drowned in the heady delights of his touch, did she understand how starved she'd been since she'd left him and how slowly time had crawled in those awful dark days.

To feel the crash of their hearts pounding so violently together through their embracing bodies...

Everything inside her bloomed wide open and light poured in.

Her stomach swooped as he lifted her into his arms.

He'd carried her like this on their wedding night, she remembered dreamily, pressing her mouth against his neck and inhaling the Massimo scent that had always made her stomach swoop all on its own.

There was such tenderness in the way he laid her down on the bed that the light that had poured inside her sparkled and glimmered through her skin and veins.

His hooded eyes glimmered too.

She could feel his hunger as keenly as she felt her own.

Gently he brushed away the locks of hair that had fallen across her face.

No words were spoken between them. No words were necessary.

She raised her hand and palmed his cheek. The bristles of his beard grazed against her skin.

Their mouths locked together.

The hand palming his cheek slipped around

his neck, her other hand sliding around his waist, pulling him down so she could feel his solid weight on her. She needed to feel that brief crush of her lungs before he shifted to release the weight, needed the assurance that she hadn't fallen into a dream.

She couldn't bear it if this was nothing but a dream. She'd suffered too many dreams in those dark days where they would be making love only for her to wake to the cold reality of a lonely bed.

There had been nightmares too, ones where he'd found someone else. One in particular had stayed with her for days. She'd been walking down the street when she'd spotted Massimo walking arm in arm with a faceless woman. She'd run after them but couldn't catch them, screaming his name as loudly as she could but no sound coming out. She'd awoken from it with a start, tears soaking into her pillow and her heart cold with a fear a hundred times worse than she'd felt in the nightmares from her childhood.

Being with him like this, here, now, evoked only warmth in her soaring heart.

She was flying.

For now, tomorrow didn't exist.

There was only now.

His hands stroked down the sides of her breasts and down to her hips where he gathered the skirt of her dress and hitched it to her waist, his mouth raining kisses over her face, her hands scratching into his scalp. They only broke away so her dress could be pulled over her head and discarded.

She saw the pulse in his eyes as he dragged his stare over her body, naked save for the skimpy black knickers she wore.

Heat flooded her with an intensity that stole her breath when he dipped his head and kissed her breasts in turn, and now it was his shirt she was scratching at, grasping to untuck it.

Every part of Livia's body had been etched in Massimo's memory but he stared at her feeling as if he were seeing it all for the first time.

His memory had played tricks on him. He'd forgotten how damned sexy she was, how perfect she was.

He'd forgotten the way her legs writhed when

she was hungry for him and to see them doing that now...

He kissed her breasts again, with more savagery than the first tender kisses he'd placed on them. He'd forgotten, too, how much she loved him lavishing attention on them. She was as receptive to his touch as he was to hers, the perfect fusion that had so blown his mind the first time they'd made love and every time after.

He moved down to her belly, divesting himself of his shirt as he went, then gripped her knickers in his fingers and pulled them down her legs to land in the pile their other clothing had formed. Working quickly, he removed the last of his own clothing too.

He could smell the musky heat of her excitement...

There was not a single thing about Livia that didn't set his blood aflame.

He kissed her thighs, digging his fingers into the pliant flesh, then ran his tongue between the soft mound of dark hair between her parted legs.

There was a clenching in his heart. Fresh

memories assailed him of the first time he'd shaved her bikini line for her and trimmed the hair. She'd been about to make an appointment at a salon when he'd suggested with a wolfish gleam that he do it for her. Her eyes had pulsed with agreement.

It had been sexy. It had been fun. The trust she had bestowed in him had blown his mind as much as everything else they had shared. After that first time they'd adopted their own language for it. It had always ended with wild lovemaking.

Her bikini line now was smooth but the rest was as nature intended. It looked to him that she hadn't bothered with it since she'd left him. For a woman who always liked to feel her best as well as look her best, right down to always wearing matching underwear that no one other than him would see, this told him everything he needed to know.

Livia hadn't been with anyone since they'd parted.

No other man had buried his face between her legs and experienced her uninhibited wild responses, the soft moans and pleas…

No other man had teased her to orgasm with his tongue alone.

He *knew* he had no right to feel such relief at this. But he did.

Livia was *his*. Just as he was hers.

Gripping her hips, he snaked his tongue back up her petite, curvy body, inhaling her skin, tasting it, nipping it, the primal eruption that had so consumed him the first time they'd made love stronger than it had ever been.

She belonged to *him*. And he belonged to her. He would always belong to her.

Elbows resting either side of her face, he gazed down in wonder. The same ragged-breath wonder reflected right back at him.

Why had he let her go? How could he have let this beautiful, sassy woman walk away without a fight?

With a groan, he plundered her plump, delectable mouth. Her arms looped around his neck and she arched her back so her breasts crushed against his chest as they devoured each other with a hungry desperation. Her legs hooked around his thighs, encouraging him, and he drove inside her in one long thrust.

The relief at being in Livia's tight, slick heat was such that he had to screw his eyes shut and drag in a breath lest he lose control immediately.

But, damn, a man could happily die like this.

Livia's head had gone. She'd lost control of her sanity when Massimo had brought her to orgasm using nothing but his tongue and now, with him sheathed so tightly inside her, the sensations were too incredible to do anything but cling tightly to him and soar in the heavenliness they were creating together.

The hummingbird that had nestled in her heart had broken free and she was flying high in the sky, reaching for the stars.

They made love with abandon, Massimo driving into her with fury tempered by tenderness, wet kisses, bites on necks, nails digging into skin, nothing existing but this moment, them, together, the fire that had always blazed so brightly between them reignited but now burning with the blue flame of desperation.

For the first time ever she found herself fighting release. She didn't want this to end.

She wanted these wonderful feelings to last for ever.

From the concentration carved on Massimo's face and the pained desire she caught every time she looked in his eyes, he was fighting the same battle.

Squeezing her eyes shut tight, she pressed her mouth into his neck and fought the growing sensations pulsating deep inside her pelvis. But it was like fighting against the tide. The pleasure was just too much...

She forgot all about fighting when the pulsations turned into an eruption that spread through her like a rippling wave. All she could do was tighten her hold on him and submit to the waves carrying her as high as the soaring hummingbird of her heart.

Livia opened her eyes with a start and immediately rolled over to check Massimo was still there. She'd fallen asleep in his arms but at some point after drifting off she must have disentangled herself.

The night was still dark but hazy light filtered in from the moon and stars. She swallowed back her relief to find his solid form lying peacefully beside her, facing her on his side. His chest rose and fell steadily.

She inched closer and covered his hand, then gently brought it up over the mattress to her lips. She razed the lightest of kisses against his knuckles and soaked in every detail of his sleeping face.

Something sharp and painful filled her chest. The hummingbird had nestled back into her heart. If Massimo opened his eyes he would see its thrumming wings beating through her skin.

She swallowed again and tried to regain control of her suddenly erratic breathing.

She pressed her mouth back against his knuckles. His fingers twitched.

Feeling herself in desperate need of air, she released his hand and slipped out of the bed. She wrapped her robe around her naked body and padded out of the bedroom.

At the back of their chalet, down the steps of their veranda, was their private garden and swimming pool. Livia sank onto a sunlounger by the pool and stared at the sun peeking over the horizon.

The cusp of a new day was showing its face but for Livia this cusp was the beginning of the end. This was the day she would say goodbye to Massimo for good…

The realisation hit her like a cold slap.

She didn't want to say goodbye.

Her feelings for Massimo were as strong as they'd ever been and the feelings he'd had for her were still there too. He'd shown it with every look, every touch and every kiss.

Why had they let that love go? Why hadn't they fought for it? The love they had once shared had been *everything*.

Massimo had slipped away from her. That was the truth. It had been so gradual that to begin with she'd only sensed it. That was what had brought her fears and insecurities out and deepened her loneliness and homesickness. Everything had escalated from that.

She talked too much but he didn't talk enough. Not about the things that were important.

That needed to change.

She looked up at the brightening sky and breathed in the warm, fragrant air. The chirrup of awakening birds sounded all around her, a joyful sound that sparked hope in her heart.

Where there was life there was hope.

What they had was worth fighting for. All she had to do was make Massimo see that too.

Filling her lungs with resolve, Livia walked back into the chalet.

If she had any chance of saving their marriage, she needed her phone, which was in the bedroom.

She pushed the door open quietly.

Massimo lifted his head. He'd woken to an empty bed. He'd registered this little fact before his eyes had opened, an emptiness where warmth should be.

He breathed a little easier to see Livia's silhouette in the doorway.

'Are you okay?' he asked, his voice croaky from sleep. He had no idea what time it was other than it was early.

It was the deepest sleep he'd had in…since she'd left him.

She stared at him for the longest time before

a smile curved over her beautiful face and she released the robe wrapped around her.

'I needed some air,' she said as she padded to the bed.

He pulled the sheets back and held his arms out for her, his body responding automatically to her unashamed nudity.

His desire for her was the one thing he'd never been able to turn off.

She nestled into his embrace.

He closed his eyes and breathed into her hair, his chest swelling. For long silent moments they did nothing but lie entwined together.

This would be the last time he held her like this.

'Why did you get spearheads added to your tattoo?' she murmured, tracing it gently with her finger before kissing it. 'I thought it was finished.'

'I thought it was finished too.'

His tattoo hadn't been finished but their marriage was.

He tightened the embrace. Regrets swirled in the air around them but it was too late for regrets. However good it felt to spend one last night with Livia, they were better off apart. They both knew that. You couldn't play on broken strings. The strings that had bound them together hadn't merely broken; they'd been irrevocably severed.

Whatever desire-driven thoughts had consumed him when they'd been making love didn't change the fact that he was better on his own. He worked better and functioned better.

Their lips found each other and the hunger that had always left him feeling starving when he was without her reared back to life.

They could have this, he thought dimly as she sank onto his length, her hair falling onto his face.

One last moment of bliss together before they said goodbye for good.

CHAPTER TEN

AFTER A LATE breakfast in the lodge, it was time to say goodbye. The guests who'd stayed the night left first until it was only Massimo, his immediate family and his grandfather's care team left.

Heart heavy, Massimo walked with them to the jetty where the cruise liner awaited. This return journey would be much shorter than the outward one. They were sailing to Viti Levu and flying to Rome from there on a private jet he'd chartered for them. After two months away from their homes, his family was looking forward to their return to Italy.

Unspoken between them all was his grandfather's health. It was the reason they were flying back. Jimmy had reserved all his energy for this stay on his birth land and his party. A two-month sail might be too late for him to have his last request of dying in his home met.

Madeline wrapped her arms around him and looked up at him with an unusually serious expression. 'Come home soon, Massimo. Please?'

Instead of the usual vague response he gave to these kinds of requests, Massimo found himself kissing his sister's cheek. 'I'll try.'

She tightened her hold. 'Try harder. We miss you.'

For the first time he found himself thinking that he *would* try.

Something had shifted in him. For all his dread at being cooped up on an island with his family, the weekend had gone much better than he'd anticipated. The more time he'd spent with them, the easier he'd found it. There had been an acceptance he'd never felt before. Or was it that he now looked at his family with fresh eyes?

Gazing over his sister's head, he saw his mother fussing with his grandfather's wheelchair. His mother loved to fuss. She was never happier than when doing things for those she loved, whether it was ironing shirts to within an inch of their lives or slaving over steaming bowls of simple home-cooked food to fill their bellies with. His father was the same too.

An old memory surfaced: sleeping on his sister's bedroom floor while his father had made a bed and wardrobe for Massimo's room. All the materials were old, reclaimed stuff but his father had made the entire lot himself right down to painting them in a colour of Massimo's choosing.

That had been his first practical exposure to the idea that something could start out as one thing and then be turned into something completely different.

Just as he was thinking that he'd finally found the root of his love of engineering and science, another memory surfaced, of the time his father found an old bicycle at a central rubbish-collection point. He'd brought it home, serviced it and painted it. By the time he presented it to Massimo—a gift for him to run his errands on—the bike looked brand new.

A wave of affection washed through him and he embraced his parents tighter than he usually did. For all the resentment he'd once felt at growing up poor, he'd never had to sleep with one ear alert to danger. He'd never had to worry about his sister being seduced into a life of crime.

After a cuddle with his niece, it was time to say goodbye to his grandfather. He sent a silent prayer that this would not be for the last time.

He watched them sail away with a weighted heart and a lump in his throat.

Beside him stood Livia, waving vigorously at his departing family.

However hard he tried to blur her from his vision she remained solid. Beautiful.

The lump that felt like granite in his throat grew. He felt all disjointed.

Abruptly, he turned on his heel and strode back down the jetty, scanning the sky for signs of the Cessna, which had taken the last of the party guests to Viti Levu and should be back by now to take Massimo and Livia to Nadi International Airport where his flight crew were waiting for them.

'Massimo?'

He closed his eyes and drew in a breath,

slowing his pace enough for Livia to catch up with him.

The last thing he wanted was a long, protracted goodbye with his wife. He had enough tumultuous feelings ripping through him.

'Are you okay?'

'Yes.'

'You've hardly spoken to me since we got out of bed. Do you regret last night?'

That was Livia. Straight to the point, as always.

'I don't regret it. I just don't see any point in talking about it.'

'We spent the night making love. I would say that gives us lots to talk about.'

That was Livia too, always so keen to discuss *feelings*, as if feelings mattered a damn.

'Last night…' He closed his eyes again and sucked in another breath, fighting the heat that spread through his veins to remember how incredible it had been. 'I'm not saying it was a mistake but, with hindsight, it shouldn't have happened.'

'Why not?'

'We're getting divorced, Liv. I know we're

going to wait for my grandfather to…' He couldn't vocalise the words. They were waiting for his grandfather to die before they went ahead with the legalities. 'It won't be long,' he finished. He didn't know if it was his grandfather's imminent death or the final severance of their marriage that caused his heart to constrict.

Dark brown eyes held his. 'Don't you have doubts?'

'Doubts?'

'About whether we're doing the right thing.'

'None.'

She flinched but didn't drop her stare. 'I do.'

'How can you have doubts?' he asked incredulously. 'This was your idea. You left *me*.'

Her slim shoulders rose. Her lips drew together before she said, 'I want to try again.'

His heart made a giant lurch. He took a step back and stared hard at her. 'One night of sex doesn't mend a broken marriage and our marriage *was* broken.'

'But we never tried to fix it. We were always too busy arguing…' She held her hands in the air. '*I* was always too busy arguing. You refused to argue. It doesn't matter who did what, the truth is we never sat down and talked and tried to find a way to fix things. We just gave up.'

'Some things can't be fixed. Our marriage is one of them and you were right to leave me. I'm sorry if last night has caused you to have doubts but—'

'Last night made me see the truth. We gave up too easily.'

'It changed nothing for me.'

Her burst of laughter sounded hollow. 'You *liar*.'

'I can't be the husband you want me to be.'

'You don't know what I want.'

'You screamed it in my face every day.'

'Then maybe you should have listened.'

'I'm not going to rehash old wounds.' He put his hand out, palm facing her; a visual sign to back up his words that he wanted this conversation to end. 'You wanted a divorce and I accepted it. It is the right thing for us to do. I'm going back to America and you're going back to Italy. That's it. Over.'

He started walking again.

'I *knew* you'd run away as soon as I brought the subject up.'

Ignoring her, he continued, craning his head to the sky again for sign of the plane. It should have been here thirty minutes ago.

'It's not coming.'

He stopped in his tracks.

'The plane. You keep looking out for it. It's not coming back today.'

Livia folded her arms across her chest and braced herself.

When he turned to look at her, his face was dark. 'What have you done?'

'I've cancelled the Cessna until tomorrow. We need to talk.'

'No, we need to go home. I have work and you have your brother waiting for you. I thought you were keen to see him and convince him that he's done the right thing in leaving.'

'He's safe,' she countered, 'and as long as he's got a gaming thing to play on and a mountain of food to eat, which he has, he won't be going anywhere. To save you time making wasted phone calls, I might as well confess that I've sent your flight crew on a sailing trip on your yacht. Even if you manage to get another Cessna to take you from the island to the mainland, you'll find it hard to leave Fiji itself.'

'What the…?' He swore loudly.

Bad language didn't faze her. She'd grown up in a home where every other word was punctuated with a curse.

His jaw clenching hard enough to snap, he pulled his phone out of his back pocket. 'I don't know what game you think you're playing but it won't work. My crew take orders from me, not from you.'

'When we married you told all your staff, flight crew included, that they were to take my orders as seriously as they took yours. Have you changed those orders?'

If looks could kill she would be dead on the ground beneath her.

'Call them if you want but you'll find they're already on the yacht drinking the champagne I ordered for them. They won't be fit to fly.' Massimo might be the undisputed brains in their marriage but when it came to planning, Livia could beat anyone. If she had any chance of getting him to stay on the island a little longer, she had to cut off all his options to leave.

Glaring at her, he punched his fingers against the screen of his phone. 'I shall charter another plane to take me home. You can stay here and rot.'

'You think you'll be able to charter a plane today? You'll be lucky to get one for tomorrow.'

'I'll take my chances.' He put his phone to his ear. A moment later he swiped it with another curse.

'If you were calling Lindy then I've already spoken to her. It's Saturday in Los Angeles...' The time difference had taken a while for Livia to get her head around but thankfully she'd found it worked in her favour. 'She's taking her daughter out for the day and keeping her phone switched off.'

'Lindy was never given instructions to obey you.'

'I asked her a favour and she agreed. It's her own private time so she's not in breach of her contract with you.'

There was a long pause of venom-filled silence.

Livia held her breath.

Then he smiled. His eyes remained blocks of ice. 'I don't need Lindy to charter a plane for me and I don't need her to book me into a hotel for the night if you're right that it's too short notice for me to charter a plane. You lose.'

'No, *we* lose,' she called to his retreating back. 'One extra day, Massimo, that's all I'm asking for. Call the flight company and have another Cessna flown in to take you off the island and check into a hotel while you wait for your flight crew to get back from their trip, or stay here with me and see if we can try and fix this marriage.'

'I am not willing to waste my energy fixing something that's beyond repair.'

'How can you say that when you've dedicated your working life on solutions for the greatest problems facing this earth that people said were beyond repair?'

'Those are problems that can be fixed by science and engineering. Our problems are fundamental.'

'I thought that about us too but now—'

Suddenly he stopped and spun round. If she

hadn't stopped walking too she would have careered into him.

'But now, *nothing*. What you have done is deplorable. I need to be back at the facility first thing Monday. We have the prototype to test...'

'Why does it have to be you?' She strove to keep her voice steady but could feel the all too familiar anger rising. 'You employ four thousand people. Are you telling me not one of them can test the prototype for you? Why can't the project manager do it?' It was an argument she'd made countless times about all the different aspects of his business.

'It's a controlled environment that I need to oversee.' It was a variation of an answer he'd given countless times too.

'The only controlled environment is your heart,' she finally snapped.

His face contorted. 'I don't have to listen to this.'

'Oh, yes, you do. If you hadn't noticed, you're stuck on an island with me. There's nowhere for you to escape unless you pay someone to get you out.' Seeing he was about to walk away again, she grabbed hold of his wrist and took a deep breath to calm her rising temper and tremulous heart. The heavy thud of his pulse against her fingers gave her the courage to continue. 'Please, Massimo, give me this one day. The Cessna's scheduled to pick us up in the morning. When it gets here, if you still want us to go our separate ways then I'll accept it but if I ever meant anything to you, and if our marriage ever meant anything to you, please, give us this chance.'

Her tight chest loosened a fraction to see a softening in the icy gaze boring into her.

He dropped his gaze to her hand and gently prised her fingers from his wrist.

'Seeing as the options you've left me mean I'm going to be a day late getting home, I need to make some calls.'

'You'll stay?' She hardly dared to hope.

He met her stare again, his expression now inscrutable. 'I'll stay but only because of the situation you've engineered. I'm not staying for us. I have no wish to be cruel but I'm not cut out for marriage. It took our marriage for me to see that.'

* * *

Massimo, sitting on the veranda at the back of the chalet, ended his final call and rubbed his fingers over his head. The testing on the prototype he'd spent the last year working on had been put back twenty-four hours, the first time he'd ever deferred anything to do with work. Livia had smashed his carefully planned schedule on its head.

Why was she doing this? Revenge for all the late nights he'd spent in his facility? This devious streak was a side of her he'd never seen before.

Surely she wasn't serious about them trying again? After everything they'd been through and everything they'd put each other through, she wanted to patch their marriage back up? The idea was ludicrous.

They *had* tried, for two long years. He couldn't make her happy then so why did she think he could make her happy now?

He pushed away the thought that the first year of their marriage had been the best of his life. That was easily explained by the high levels of dopamine and other hormones induced by great sex.

He should never have made love to her last night. That was what had brought all this stupid, devious behaviour from her on. The hormones released by their lovemaking had messed with his head too but in the bright light of day the fog his brain had succumbed to had cleared and he could see with clarity again.

He hoped his blunt parting words had given her some much-needed clarity too.

A burst of frustration shot through him and, without thinking, he threw his phone onto the veranda's terracotta tiles. If not for the protective case around it, it would have shattered.

Scowling at the phone as if it were its own fault that it was on the ground, he got off his chair and reached down to pick it back up. As his fingers closed around it a pair of bare feet with pretty painted toenails appeared before him. Attached to the feet was a pair of smooth, bare legs, a scar running along the calf of one, attached to a curvy body wrapped in a sheer pale blue sarong beneath which Livia was very obviously naked. Her newly cut and highlighted chestnut hair was piled high on top of her head, locks spilling over a large pair of aviator shades.

He straightened, his foul mood deepening at the spark of response that flashed through his loins and darkening to see the bucket she carried under her arm, which had a bottle of champagne in it, and the two champagne flutes she held by the stems.

Seemingly oblivious to her presence being unwelcome, she placed everything carefully on the table without speaking and poured the champagne into the flutes. Then she had a large drink from one and removed her shades. Her eyes didn't even flicker at him.

Still not speaking, she then turned around and walked to the steps that led down to their private garden and pool. Before going down the steps, she paused.

He held his breath.

The sarong dropped to the ground.

He clamped his lips tightly together to smother the groan that formed in his throat.

What was she playing at now?

Whatever it was, he would not play along.

But he could not tear his eyes from the nymph-like form.

Her naked bottom swayed gently as she made her way slowly...seductively...down the steps to the thick, green lawn. When she reached the pool she dipped a toe in the water, then entered the pool, wading into it from the wide, gently sloping steps in the arch of the shallow end until she was waist deep. And then she began to swim, a slow breaststroke.

There was no suppressing the groan from his throat at the first frog kick of her legs.

Livia swam to the end of the pool and stopped. The water being only chest deep here, she pressed her hands together on the pool's ledge, rested her chin on them and stared out at the softly rippling waves of the ocean lapping only metres from the edge of the private garden and enjoyed the feel of the sun baking her skin.

Massimo's reaction to her entrapping him on the island hadn't surprised her but it had still hurt. But, whatever he'd said about not being cut out for marriage, she wasn't about to raise a white flag and admit defeat. She knew he still had feelings for her. She just had to break down his barriers for him to see that, with a little compromise and a lot of effort, they could have the life together they'd once dreamed of.

The barriers she'd erected to protect herself had been demolished in one blissful night. What did she have to lose?

Being here this weekend, with the man she loved and with the family she wished she could have had for her own… It had brought back everything she'd wanted for them, everything they'd had at the beginning of their marriage. Gentle teasing. Mutual support. Fun. Laughter. Love.

If she failed, at least she could look herself in the eye and say she'd tried. At least she'd be able to move on rather than being stuck in the awful limbo she'd spent the past four months existing in.

She sensed movement behind her before she heard it. Her heart began to thud but she didn't move, not even when the water rippled around her.

CHAPTER ELEVEN

MASSIMO FELT AS if he'd been drugged.

He'd kept his gaze fixed on Livia, telling himself again and again that he wouldn't play her game.

He'd still been telling himself that when he'd stripped his clothes off.

He'd still been telling himself that when he'd stepped into the water and swum to her.

She made no effort to acknowledge him, not even when he stood behind her.

His hands working of their own volition, he reached into her hair and pulled the pin holding it together out.

Her right shoulder made the smallest of movements but she still didn't acknowledge him.

Her hair tumbled down.

He smoothed it with his hands then pressed

his nose into the fragrant silk while dragging his fingers down her back and then sliding them around her waist. 'Why did you cut it?' he murmured.

She leaned back into him with a soft sigh and moved her hands to slide them over his arms. Her nails scratched through the fine hairs of his forearms as her bottom wriggled provocatively against his arousal.

He slid his hand over her ribcage and cupped a weighty breast. His blood had thickened so much that even his heart felt sluggish within the heavy beats.

The small hands pulled away from his arms and reached up behind her shoulders, her fingers groping for him. And then she twisted around to face him.

Her breasts brushed against his chest, her abdomen pressed against his arousal, her hands cupped his neck.

Colour heightened her face, the dark eyes black with desire, the plump lips parted...

Those lips...

Mouths fused together in a kiss of hard, passionate savagery as the desire between them unleashed like a coil springing free from its tight box.

This was how it had always been between them, he thought, in the hazy recess of his mind. One touch had always been enough to ignite the torch that blazed so brightly between them.

Gripping her hips, he lifted her from the water to place her bottom onto the pool's ledge, parted her legs with his thighs, and thrust straight inside her welcoming heat.

She gasped into his mouth then kissed him even harder.

His fingers digging into her hips, her fingers digging into his neck and scalp, mouths clashing together, he drove in and out of her, fast, furious, thrusting as deep as he could go, pain and pleasure driving them on and on to a climax that had her crying his name and Massimo finding himself separating from his body in a wash of brilliant colour.

It took a long time to come back to himself.

He barely remembered climbing out of the pool and collapsing into an entwined heap of naked limbs on the soft lawn. The afternoon sun above blazed down on them, its heat tempered by the breeze coming from the ocean.

'We should get some sunscreen on you,' he muttered.

Her lips pressed into his neck before she clambered upright and got to her feet. 'Don't go anywhere. I'll be back in a minute.'

When she'd disappeared from view, he rolled onto his back and stretched his limbs with a long sigh.

Slinging an arm across his forehead, he closed his eyes. There was a lethargy within him. His heart still thumped heavily.

He should get up and put his clothes back on before Livia came back with the sunscreen.

He knew what he *should* do. The trouble was his lethargic limbs refused to cooperate, just as his limbs had refused his mind's instructions not to play her sensual game in the pool.

His body had been Livia's slave from the moment they'd met.

He wanted to be angry with her for using her sexuality as a weapon against him but he couldn't. He understood what she was doing. His anger was directed at himself.

When she returned wearing her sarong and carrying two full flutes of champagne whilst also balancing the sunscreen and a couple of beach towels under her arm, he rolled onto his side and propped himself on his elbow.

'Livia, I'm sorry...'

'But this doesn't change anything?' she finished for him with a raised brow. She put the champagne and towels on the poolside table and removed her sarong.

'It's okay, Massimo,' she said as she spread the sarong out like a blanket on the lawn. 'Sometimes great sex is just that—great sex. Could you do my back for me, please?'

Livia sat with her legs stretched out on the sarong and waited for him to join her on it.

Massimo, she had discovered early on in their relationship, opened up more easily after sex, when his defences were down in the wave of euphoria that followed it.

She knew stripping naked and seducing him visually could be considered as fighting dirty but there was no shame in seducing her own husband. They both took great pleasure from making love. If she could go back in time and do one thing differently it would be to stop herself turning her back on him in the last months of their marriage. Without sex to keep the intimacy between them alive, the glue that had held them together had disintegrated. There had been nothing left.

But sex wasn't all a marriage could or should be and intimacy came in many forms.

She leaned forward, hugging her knees when he put his hands filled with sunscreen on her back.

Unlike when he'd worked the screen into her skin briskly on the yacht, he took his time. His touch was soothing. She closed her eyes to savour the sensation.

'What did I do to turn you away from me?' she asked quietly.

His hands paused in their work. 'I don't know what you mean.'

'Yes, you do. You turned away from me, Massimo. You stopped caring. Even if tomorrow you decide everything's still over for us, I need to know because the not knowing's killing me.'

Massimo clenched his jaw and breathed in deeply.

What was the point in discussing something that wouldn't make the slightest difference to anything? But she'd steered it so he had no choice. If she'd shouted her demands as she'd always done, he would happily walk away, as he always used to. But she was using temperance. Using the closeness of sex.

He rubbed the sunscreen into her lower back and forced his mind to disassociate from the soft skin beneath his fingers. 'You didn't do anything. We're just not suited. My work is my life. There isn't the space for anything more.'

'You didn't think that when we got together.'

'My feelings for you took me by surprise.' They'd floored him. 'I let those feelings guide me instead of sitting down and thinking them through rationally. You and I have a rare chemistry but, when you boil it down, it's nothing but adrenaline, dopamine, oxytocin, serotonin…'

'Do not reduce my feelings to a chemistry lesson.' An edge crept into her voice.

Good. The dopamine currently flowing through her needed to be extinguished.

'All the effects of desire and what we think of as love can be reduced to a chemical level,' he explained levelly. 'The overwhelming feelings we experience at the start of a relationship are a surge of chemical reactions but those chemicals are raised to unsustainable levels. Eventually they lessen, which is what happened to us.'

'Nice try at deflection but what happened to us is that you turned away from me.' She leaned forward and traced her finger along the scar on her leg. 'This cut was when I really felt it. You didn't care that I was injured.'

'I did care but you told me it wasn't anything serious.' But his first instinct had been to grab his keys and speed straight to her. That had been the day after he'd realised how far behind they were on the carbon filter project because of basic errors *he'd* made. The first errors he'd made in his entire career. The day after he'd woken Livia from a nightmare and held her trembling body tightly to him and found himself developing his own cold sweat at how badly he'd wanted to dive into her head and rip out the terrors that plagued her.

That had been the moment he'd understood what a dreadful mistake he'd made.

The fun, sexy marriage he'd envisaged for them had become an all-consuming sickness in his blood. Livia had taken full possession of his mind as well as his body.

He'd *had* to back away. Before he lost everything.

If she had given him the space he needed things might have been very different but she hadn't and a gulf had opened between them that had only solidified how wrong they were for each other.

'I didn't want to worry you because I thought you would drive to me,' she said wistfully. 'When we first married, I slipped and bumped my head one evening. Do you remember that? It wasn't anything serious but you stayed home the next day to keep an eye on me. You were worried about concussion even though I'm a nurse and told you there was nothing to worry about. Less than a year later you sent your PA to drive me to hospital with a gashed leg.'

He'd sent his PA after first having to prise

his car keys from his own hands to drop them in Lindy's palm.

He shifted away from Livia's smooth, golden back and got to his feet. 'Do you have any idea how much work I missed in the first year of our marriage and how behind we got because of it?' He snatched up one of the beach towels she'd left on the poolside table. 'This carbon filter we're about to test should have been ready months ago.'

'That's because you have to micromanage everything.'

He secured the towel around his waist. 'It's my company.'

Her eyes found his. If she felt at a disadvantage remaining naked while he'd covered himself, she didn't show it. 'You employ some of the world's biggest brains. If you can't trust their skills and judgement then what does that say? It says you're either a control freak or you need to employ people who you do trust.'

'No, it says I take my responsibilities seriously.'

'You're in the position where you can allow others who are equally responsible and qualified to share the burden. You choose not to. You use the excuse of your work to cut yourself off from everyone who loves you and you still haven't explained why you cut yourself away from me. We were *happy*, Massimo. We were. And then we had nothing and I need to understand why and, please, for the love of God, don't explain it to me as a scientific formula. I get that we're nothing but atoms and dust but we're also conscious beings who feel and love and dream.'

Feeling in better control of himself, he took a seat at the poolside table and drank his champagne in one deep swallow. Bourbon would have numbed the agitation growing in his stomach much better but this would do.

He had to make her understand. Whatever delusions Livia had allowed herself to believe, he needed to dispel them. Since she'd left him, his world had reverted to its prior orderly calm. His time was where it needed to be—with his business. His mind was clutter-free. The stupid errors that had crept into his work were relegated to history. His wife would soon be relegated to history too. Everything would be as it should be.

'It's just the way I am. I was always different from the rest of my family.' Damn but he really could do with a bourbon. 'They didn't care if the clothes they wore were fraying at the seams or if there wasn't the money available to fix things that broke but I did. They think love alone can fix everything when in reality only hard work achieves anything. I love them in my own way but I never felt as if I belonged and I never wanted to settle for making do. I didn't set out to be rich but I did set out to be well off enough that I would never want for anything.'

Livia pounced on his choice of words. 'You love them in your own way? That implies you're aware of feeling love on something other than a chemical level.'

His eyes narrowed. 'You're twisting my words against me.'

'No, I'm pointing out your hypocrisy. You know perfectly well that love, however it is formed, is real but you're using science as an excuse to deny that what you and I had was real. I never had shoes with holes or clothes that didn't fit but, given the choice, I would have suffered that than live through my childhood. My father was always generous with his money and gave me everything I asked for but I was terrified of him.'

There was the barest flicker in the shuttered caramel eyes but it was enough for the faint hope in her heart to continue beating. 'Whenever he hugged me, all I felt was his gun digging into my chest from his pocket. When he was killed, I was upset because he was my father but I never grieved him like the rest of my family did because the bogeyman of my early childhood *was* my father. My mother was hardly ever there and when she was she would be high or drunk. I practically raised Gianluca—I was the one who took him to school every day and helped him with his homework and made sure he had a hot meal at night.

'Your parents are decent, law-abiding, loving people.' If she was going to fight, she might as well fight on his family's behalf too. But it wasn't just a fight for herself or for the Briatores. She was fighting for Massimo, for him to wake up and see all the joy of love and family that he was denying himself. She got to her feet and gathered the sarong as she continued, 'They could have worked longer hours or taken additional jobs to give you everything you wanted but they made the choice to be there for you whenever you needed them and I wish I could make you see how priceless that was.'

'From your perspective, anyone else's childhood would be priceless.'

'Maybe,' she conceded, wrapping the sarong around her. 'But we're talking about our own, not anyone else's. You are very different from your family but there are similarities. You have their generosity but yours is given in material ways where theirs is given in time.'

His fingers curved on the table but his eyes remained fixed on her. 'I cannot un-live my childhood just because yours was, on a sliding scale, much worse. It made me who I am. It taught me that anything I wanted or needed, I had to get by myself. My parents loved me, yes, but their love didn't change the reality of us being poor. It didn't solve anything. You could be right. I could be a control freak. But everything I have has been achieved by my own endeavours. Science is logical and it's real. It's where I feel most comfortable. It's where I belong but to do my best work, I need my mind to be free from clutter.'

It took her a moment to process the implication of what he'd just said. 'Are you calling me *clutter*?'

His response was unapologetic. 'You became a distraction. You demanded my attention when I needed to be focused.'

'All I ever *demanded* was your time.' Try as she might, she couldn't hide the rising anger. 'Since when is it a crime to want to spend time with your own husband?'

'That is my point perfectly encapsulated. I cannot produce my best work when I'm constantly worrying about you. I need to be free to focus without limits, not clock-watching, not worrying about you being lonely at home, not thinking I need to drive home because you're waiting for me with your dinner going cold.'

'My food wouldn't have gone cold if you'd

bothered to let me know you were going to be late,' she retorted.

'That was never intentional.'

'And now you're contradicting yourself again. If it wasn't intentional you wouldn't have worried about it.'

Over the still air, Massimo's ringtone suddenly played out. He looked from Livia to the table on the veranda and back to her.

She gritted her teeth. 'Please. Leave it.'

But of course he wouldn't leave it. It might be *important*. Far more important than her and their marriage.

He strode away without a backwards glance.

She suspected bitterly that he would have cut their conversation short to answer it even if it were a cold caller.

Massimo had set himself up in a shaded part of the veranda, laptop open before him and his phone wedged to his ear. Furious with his retreat from their conversation and his deliberate immersion back into his work, Livia knew she needed to create a little distance between them before she snatched his phone off him and chucked it into the ocean. Doing that would only make things worse. If they could get any worse.

Of the many stories Jimmy had told her about his childhood on this island, the one that had fed Livia's imagination the most had been tales of the Seibua children playing in the naturally formed freshwater pool hidden in the thick forest. When she'd taken Jimmy for an exploration of the island, he'd pointed in the direction of its location and it was with that in mind, and conscious that the sun would soon begin its descent, that she set off.

By the time she passed the lodge, her fury had dimmed a little, enough for her to pass a message to Massimo through one of the staff members of where she was going. Just in case he missed her. Which he wouldn't, a knowledge that curdled her belly with bitter misery.

Her head streamed their conversation continually as she reached the red mangrove saplings planted at the edge of the shore; it echoed as she made her way inland past the black mangroves, which Massimo had explained were protection against the shallow flooding that occurred at high tide, still burred in her ears as she strode upwards to the white mangroves and onwards to the butterwoods until she reached the island's natural forest.

The pathway the Seibua children had taken had disappeared long ago but she'd walked in as straight a direction as she could and she was sure she would find it. If not, she'd go back.

Here, under the natural canopy of trees, the vegetation was dense with colourful wildlife and rich with sound. The heat was stifling but she didn't care. Large red-chested sociable parrots chattered noisily in squeaks and whistles, other less visible birds adding to the wonderful cacophony. None of them seemed bothered by her presence.

Soon, just as Jimmy had described, the canopy began to thin until she was standing in a small, sandy clearing centred around a startlingly clear pool of water no bigger than their private swimming pool. It was like stepping into a magical fairy tale.

She stood still for a moment to inhale the fresher air and enjoy the feel of the light wind on her face. At the water's edge two coconut palms stood tall and proud, their fronds dancing to the breeze's rhythm.

The last of her anger left her as she noticed the distinctive red heads and bright green bodies of Fiji Parrotfinches bathing happily in the pool. She wouldn't be surprised if a couple of deer and rabbits appeared and began communicating with her.

Livia removed her sandals and sat carefully on the stony wall encasing the pool. The Fiji Parrotfinches were not prepared to tolerate this and flew off back into the surrounding forest, leaving her in silence.

Her thoughts weren't silent though. They were screaming their rising desperation and panic in her ears.

Foolishly, she'd hoped Massimo would at least consider giving their marriage another try. The happiness they'd once shared…that had been *real*.

Why hadn't she fought sooner? There had been so much to fight for but they had both let it descend into cold acrimony. She bore as much responsibility for this as Massimo. Livia knew how to fight. Fighting was one thing she excelled at. She could shout and scream and stamp her feet but she hadn't done the most important thing, which was to listen. When he'd asked for space and peace she'd taken it personally. She'd allowed her insecurities and fears to take root. Instead of giving him what he'd asked for she'd pushed even harder.

Exhaustion washed through her. What did all this even matter? How could she fight for a marriage when her husband didn't see anything worth saving? He'd had a taste of life without her and found it preferable.

Oh, God, the *pain* that ripped through her. And then the panic. It was all there in her battered, frightened heart as the depth of her love finally screamed unfiltered to the surface.

Massimo was the love of her life. How could she ever sleep again if he slipped away for good? How could she ever breathe properly?

The tears that had threatened to unleash since she'd woken in his arms filled her eyes. She no longer had the strength to hold them back.

Hugging her knees to her chest, Livia bowed her head and wept.

CHAPTER TWELVE

THE SKY HAD turned golden when Massimo disappeared under the canopy of trees.

He hadn't planned to go in search of Livia. He'd fixed the business problem that had cropped up and had intended to keep working but the silence Livia had left when she'd slipped away without a word had been louder than the ocean. It had deafened him. Every time he'd looked at his laptop, nothing had penetrated his brain.

The disjointed feelings had returned with a vengeance.

He'd decided a brisk walk on the fine white sandy beach was in order but he'd barely taken ten paces when one of his workers had rushed up to tell him Livia had gone off in search of the freshwater pool in the forest.

He'd shrugged the message off and walked

another ten paces when an image of Livia lost and alone in the forest had formed in his head. He'd performed an abrupt about-turn.

Mercifully, the worker knew exactly where the pool was located.

The forest canopy cast everything in shadow and he increased his pace, praying he was heading in the right direction and not meandering from the route.

How long had she been here? She'd walked away from their chalet a couple of hours ago. Had she even found the pool? The island was small but the forest was dense and large enough to lose yourself in.

Perspiration clung to his skin when he finally found the clearing but he didn't know if it was from the heat or the fear that had gripped his heart. The sky had turned a deeper orange in his time in the forest. There was little daylight left.

He exhaled a long breath of relief to see her there. She was sitting with her feet in the pool gazing down into the water.

On legs that felt strangely unsteady, he stepped over and crouched beside her.

Other than a long, defeated sigh, she made no reaction to his presence.

He followed her gaze to peer into the still, clear water. He couldn't see what had captivated her attention so greatly.

Long moments passed before she turned her face to him.

He sucked in a shocked breath.

Even under the fading light he could see the puffiness of her red eyes. Her cheeks and neck were blotchy.

'Have you been crying?' he asked in a hoarse voice.

Eyes dark with misery met his. Her pretty nose wriggled, her chin wobbled and her shoulders shook before her face crumpled and tears fell like a waterfall down her face.

Massimo froze.

Not once in the entirety of their marriage had he seen his wife cry.

A tiny fissure cracked in his heart.

Working on autopilot, he twisted round to take her into his arms and held her tightly. She clung to him, sobbing into his chest, her hot tears soaking his T-shirt.

Something hot and sharp stabbed the back of his eyes and he blinked violently to clear it.

'Tell me what the matter is,' he urged, kissing the top of her head and strengthening his hold around her. Livia's vulnerability was something he'd always sensed rather than seen, something she'd always striven to mask. To witness her like this, with all her barriers and defences stripped away...

The fissure in his heart splintered into a thousand crevices all filling with an emotion so painful it felt as if his insides were splitting into pieces.

Her shoulders shook and she slowly raised her face to look at him. There was a despairing quality when she whispered his name before the ghost of a smile flittered on her tear-drenched lips. 'For such a clever man you can be incredibly stupid.'

He never got the chance to ask what she meant for her lips found his and he was pulled into a kiss of such hungry desperation that his senses responded before his brain could stop it.

Desperation had formed in his own skin too, an agonising ache of need for the woman whose tears hurt him in a place he'd never known existed.

In a crush of arms they tumbled to the sandy ground. There was no attempt or need for seduction or foreplay, that hungry ache to be as one all-consuming. Deep inside him breathed a wish to crawl into Livia's skin and rip out every demon that had filled his beautiful, strong wife with such desolation.

Together, their hands tugged frantically at his shorts and her bikini bottoms, anguished passion there in every touch and every kiss.

They clung to each other as he drove deep inside her, their mouths crushed together, bodies fused tightly. There was a hopeless urgency in their lovemaking he had never experienced before and it flowed through them both, every soft moan of pleasure from her mouth a cry, every gasp a sob, a feeling in his soul that his world was on the verge of collapse, all of it combining to heighten the pleasure and shadow it with despair.

Only the despair racked him when it was over and the heady sensations had seeped away from him.

But his heart still thumped painfully when he pulled away from her and covered his face.

This had to stop.

They were over. *Over.*

Why prolong the pain? Hadn't they hurt each other enough?

Long moments passed in heavy silence before he rolled onto his side and got to his feet. Pulling his shorts on, he muttered, 'It's getting dark. We should get back.'

She didn't answer, simply rearranged her clothing and ran her fingers through her hair. As she did so, he noticed something that made him pause, perplexed. One of her nails was missing...

He snatched at the diversion from all the weight crushing him. 'What happened to your nail?'

She shrugged. 'It fell off.'

'They're false?'

She nodded.

He had no idea why this disturbed him so much. 'Since when do you wear false nails?'

More to the point, since when did she *bite* her nails?

Livia had always taken pride in her nails. Even when she'd worked as a nurse and been forced to keep them short for practical reasons they'd been buffed and polished. This nail was so short and ragged the nail bed was exposed.

She shrugged again. 'They needed doing.'

Shrugging the subject away with the same indifference she'd dismissed it with, Massimo reached into his pocket for his phone and turned the torch app on. It was bright enough to lead them back through the forest in relative safety but, all the same, he made sure to keep Livia close to him as they headed back along the route he'd taken to reach her, resisting the urge to take her hand.

No more touching her. He would dine alone and sleep in a cabin far from her. Far from the temptation he'd proven himself incapable of resisting.

But those tears…

Where had they come from? Surely she hadn't been crying about them?

It disturbed him to recall how close he'd come to tears too. He hadn't cried since he was a small child.

When they emerged from the forest and into the young mangroves, the first stars had emerged in the night sky.

Livia looked up at them and wished their shining brilliance could penetrate Massimo's heart and make him see that what they had could shine with that same brilliance too.

The incoming tide had covered most of the beach and she sat on the stone wall that acted as a barrier and looked up again at the vast night sky.

She had no idea what the time was.

Time was slipping away from her as fast as Massimo was.

Her fight to save them was a fight she was losing. She could feel it in her soul.

She could still taste their lovemaking on her lips but here he was now, sitting beside her at a distance that meant she would have to stretch her arm out to touch him.

'Did you know I fell in love with your family before I fell in love with you?' she said into the still air. 'Before I met them, I was stone inside. I'd had to fight and work for everything I had, escaping the Secondigliano, getting into nurs-

ing, supporting myself through my degree…
even getting my placement in oncology so I
could be a cancer nurse was a battle. Keeping
myself detached while not losing my compassion for my patients and their families was a
constant fight.'

She'd worked hard and fought her entire life.
But her marriage? She'd thrown that away with
hardly a whimper and now she feared she'd
left it too late to repair it.

He shifted, stretching his legs out. The lapping tide drew in inches from his toes.

'Your grandfather was the first patient I ever
became attached to. His home was so *warm*.
All those photos of you all everywhere…' She
sighed to remember the feelings being in that
home had brought about in her. Jimmy had
been her third private placement after she'd
been head-hunted by the agency to work as a
private oncology nurse. 'I was used to family
members dropping in for regular short visits with the other placements, but your family were always there. They fed him, watched
television with him, read to him. They lifted
his spirits better than any medicine. The love

they all had for each other opened my eyes to what a family should be like: built on love and support and just being there for each other. I wanted that so badly I could taste it. And then I met you...'

She clasped her hands together, remembering how it had felt to lie naked and cocooned in Massimo's arms that first night, the beat of his strong heart thudding against her... Nothing had ever felt more right in her life.

It made her soul weep to think she might never feel that rightness again.

'I fell so *hard* for you,' she whispered. 'When you proposed, I imagined a family life like the one your family had. I imagined babies and lots of visits to and from your parents. I assumed your detachment from them was a result of you being a single man living on the other side of the ocean and that once we were married you would want to spend more time with them. It took me a long time to realise that my assumptions had been delusional.' She filled her lungs with the fresh salty air. 'I could have coped with all that if you hadn't started detaching yourself from *me*. It scared me, Massimo. I could feel you slipping away and I didn't know how to bring you back and I made everything worse with my reaction to it all. I knew you didn't respond well to confrontation but I still kept on confronting you because that's the only way I knew to deal with things. Growing up was a survival of the fittest. If someone upset you, you confronted them. You learned to never show weakness. To back down made you weak and made you a target. I try so hard not to be that woman any more.'

Those confrontational traits had become her default position, a cycle she hadn't known how to break out of.

'You have two ears and one mouth for a reason,' Massimo had once said to her on one of the rare times she'd been able to spark a reaction out of him.

Those were words she'd carried every day since she'd left him.

She'd stopped supporting him in his work. She'd become *resentful* of his work. All the wonderful qualities she'd fallen in love with... she'd forgotten them because he'd hidden them away. He'd turned into a recluse from her and she in turn had become a shrill person she despised.

Fresh tears welled behind her eyes.

She let them fall.

There was nothing to hide any more. This was her, stripped bare of the things she always kept locked away from him, the vulnerabilities she'd hidden as she'd always hidden them since she was too young to even know what vulnerability meant.

'I remember us going to that technology awards ceremony you were guest of honour at. I got talking to one of the other trophy wives…'

'You were *never* a trophy wife,' he interrupted tightly.

'Not to begin with but that's how I felt in the second year. The wife I was talking to asked me how many lovers you'd had since we'd married. You should have seen her face when I said none. She thought I was delusional. All rich men have lovers. But not you. I never doubted you. Even when you spent nights in your office rather than come home to me, I never once had suspicions you were seeing other women. It would have been easier to compete with a flesh and blood woman but your mistress was always your business and I grew resentful towards it. I hate myself for walking away and not fighting harder for us. I hate that I became so needy and resentful. We could have the marriage we once dreamed about but we both have to want it and work at it.'

Massimo had never felt the thuds of his heart as clearly as he did right then. The crash they made in his ears reverberated with the distant crash of waves and sluiced through his entire being.

'But that's the problem,' he said harshly. 'I don't want it. We did try, Liv, but it wasn't enough then and it wouldn't be enough now. You might not want to hear about our marriage being reduced to a scientific formula but everything that drove us to marry in the first place was because of the heightened chemicals overpowering our rationality. What you're feeling now is a reignition of those chemicals brought about by—'

'Don't you *dare*,' she interrupted with a tearful edge. 'Don't tell me what I feel. I *know* what I feel. I love you. I'm well aware that the early days of a relationship are driven by heightened emotions and hormones—that's what normal people call the honeymoon period—but for you to keep reducing the love we shared to science is an insult to every memory we created together. If you simply stopped loving me, at least have the guts to say so.'

Nausea swirled violently inside him. 'I don't know if what I felt for you was love or not. I don't know if it was real. The feelings I had for you were the strongest I have ever felt but you must see that even if it was love, it doesn't solve anything. The problems we had would still be there eating away at us.'

'I don't see that. Not if we're both prepared to work at it.' The hitch in her voice made his heart contract but he made himself stay focused and strong.

This was for the best. One day, when the intensity of everything they'd shared these last few days had subsided, she would see that too.

'I'm afraid that I do see it like that,' he said

in as even a voice as he could manage. 'I'm not prepared to return to a marriage that's a proven failure. I'm not prepared to put myself through that again. It isn't worth it.'

There was a moment of silence until, without any warning, she jumped off the wall and waded out into the ocean until she was standing thigh high in the water. The moon had risen, bathing her in a silvery glow.

'Do you know what I don't understand?' Her voice carried through the breeze and the waves. 'How you can work so hard to save the world we live in when you've no intention of enjoying anything it has to offer. And I don't see or understand how you can put your mind to *anything* and make it succeed when you won't put a fraction of that energy into saving our marriage.'

'A marriage is not a business.'

'You're right. A marriage involves feelings. A business won't care for you when you're sick or lonely.' She rolled her neck and turned. Treading slowly through the water, she seemed to become magnified as she neared him.

The expression on her face sent coldness snaking up his spine and through his veins.

'You might not think our love *worth* it or know if it was real or not but I do. My love was real. I left you and I fell to pieces. I don't know what was worse—living with the ghost you'd become or living without you. Being apart from you felt like I'd had my heart ripped out. Every day was a battle just to get out of bed. I have no idea how I kept the charade going when I visited your family or Gianluca.' As she spoke, her voice grew steadily colder to match the expression on her face. 'I don't care what you think about your feelings for me but don't you ever lie to yourself that my love for you was anything but pure. You were my whole world. I gave up everything to be with you but I wasn't even worth fighting for, was I? You just breathed a great sigh of relief to be rid of me and got on with your life. My God, I've been *pathetic.*'

She took a step back and brought the hand with the missing nail to her face and stared at it as if she were seeing it for the first time before looking back at him. 'I'm no better than my mother. She would sit at the kitchen table late at night biting her nails while she waited for my father to come home.'

Massimo had seen many emotions from Livia in their time together but this was the first time she'd ever looked at him with contempt.

'And you're no better than my father.'

As insults went, that was the worst she could have thrown at him. A hot cauldron of anger rose in him. 'Do not compare me to that man.'

'His work, if you can call it that, came first in his life, just as yours does.'

Rising to his feet, Massimo flexed his hands and leaned forward to speak right into her face. 'Your father was killed in a gangland shooting. That was his work. You dare compare it to mine? My work has the potential to save the world from catastrophe!'

'And that's all that matters to you,' she spat back but still in the same controlled voice. 'Your work. At least my father loved his family.'

'Love?' He burst into a roar of incredulous laughter. 'You were terrified of him!'

'I was terrified because he was a monster but even monsters can love their family. He loved us and he wasn't afraid to show it but you... You shut out everyone who loves you. You want to know why I cut my hair?' She turned and parted her hair at the back of her scalp.

His heart throbbing madly, his guts cramped, confounded and disjointed that his temper was fraying at the seams while Livia had hers under such tight control, he blinked rapidly and leaned forward to see what she was showing him. Even with only the moon and the stars to illuminate them, he could see the exposed section she'd parted contained a small bald patch.

'Stress-induced alopecia,' she explained tightly, releasing her hair as she looked back at him. 'I had it cut and layered to cover it when I had my nails done last week because my pride couldn't bear for you to look at me and think I'd suffered in any way without you. I was trying to prove to myself, too, that I was over you and now I know I am because all the love I had for you...you've just killed it.'

His nausea had returned with a vengeance. 'Livia…'

'I don't want to hear any more of your excuses.' Her eyes blazed with a hardness he'd never seen before, a look he instinctively knew she hadn't given since leaving Naples. 'I'm not *prepared…*' she dragged the word out with a sneer '…to waste another atom of energy on a man who refuses to give me an inch of what he devotes to his business. Enjoy the rest of your life—I hope you and your business are very happy together.'

The footprints she made in the sand as she walked away with her head held high were covered by foaming ocean within moments of being created.

CHAPTER THIRTEEN

THE RETURN JOURNEY was harder than the outbound journey had been. Livia had debated the idea of making her own way back to Italy but reluctantly decided against it. It would take twice as long as it would to fly with Massimo and she wanted to be at home with her brother.

She had walked away from him with her head held high and kept her own company since, her emotions veering from humiliation to anger and back again. The only emotion she wouldn't allow herself was despair.

Her anger was directed only at herself.

She *had* been pathetic. Not only in her marriage but in the aftermath, after she'd walked away. When she should have reclaimed her life and moved on, she'd become stuck in purgatory, unable to sever the emotional ties that had kept her bound to Massimo.

They were severed now.

Their only communication since her disastrous attempt at reconciliation had been a text message from him that morning informing her they would be leaving the island in ten minutes.

She'd spent the night in Madeline's chalet. She neither knew nor cared where Massimo had slept.

During the short flight on the Cessna to Nadi airport, she'd refused to look at him and rebuffed his few attempts at conversation. When they'd boarded his jet, she'd taken her original seat, stuck her earphones in and selected the most mindless movie she could find.

The moment they were in the air, she'd put the physical barrier around her seat up. It went perfectly with the metaphorical barrier she'd erected.

The one good thing about this return journey was that Massimo would only be travelling as far as LA with her. She had no doubt he would go straight to his precious facility.

When one of the cabin crew asked if she would like something to eat she readily accepted and forced the warm baguette filled with smoked cheese and prosciutto into her cramped stomach.

She would never allow her feelings to prevent her from eating ever again.

She had no idea if Massimo ate. She refused to look.

She still refused to look at him when they landed in LA, even when he hovered by her seat as if trying to get her attention.

'Take care of yourself,' he muttered after she'd ignored him for as long as he could tolerate.

And then he was gone.

She didn't expel a breath until he'd left the cabin.

The baguette she'd eaten felt as if it wanted to expel itself out of her system. She held it down and left the plane too, escorted by a hefty security guard to a private lounge. She didn't have to worry about bumping into Massimo. He would already be in his car.

But he wasn't in his car.

Livia's heart came to a shuddering halt when the lounge door opened a few minutes later and Massimo stood at the threshold looking paler than she'd ever seen him.

She knew what was wrong before he spoke, her heart already aching for him before the words came out.

'My grandfather had a bad turn on the flight home. They don't think he's going to make it.'

The only illumination in the room Massimo sat in came from the machines hooked to his grandfather's weakening body. The incessant beeping from them grated in his head like nails on a chalkboard.

He'd shifted the armchair as close to the bed as he could get it. His parents were sleeping in a spare room down the corridor. The medical team were resting in the adjoining room. His sister had gone home for the night, making Massimo promise to call her if anything changed.

Nothing had changed in the two days his grandfather had been home. Nothing apart from his steadily weakening heart.

Jimmy Seibua was dying. But he was dying in the home he loved. His bedroom had been turned into its own hospital room with everything needed to keep him comfortable and pain-free until nature finally took its course.

The door opened.

He didn't need to look to know it was Livia. He would know her movements blindfolded.

'Hot chocolate,' she said softly.

He took one of the steaming cups from her with a muted thanks.

She placed her own cup on a ledge before pulling a thermometer from the dedicated medical cupboard and running it gently over his grandfather's forehead. After logging the reading and checking the equipment he was hooked to, she pulled the other armchair closer and sat beside Massimo. 'He's comfortable. That's the most important thing.'

Massimo nodded.

In the two days they'd been holed up in his grandfather's home, Livia had left only once, a short trip to her apartment on the other side of the city to check in on her brother.

He could never put into words how grateful he was to have her there. Her calm, compassionate presence soothed his family's nerves.

It soothed his nerves too. She could easily save her compassion for the rest of his family and pretend he didn't exist but she didn't.

'How are you doing?' she asked quietly.

He shrugged. He didn't know how he was doing. He felt battered from the inside.

'Have you eaten?'

'I'm not hungry.'

Her small hand rested on his and gave a gentle squeeze. It lasted only seconds but it spread a little warmth into his cold veins.

He had to stop himself from reaching over to snatch her hand back and keep it tucked in his.

She stayed with him for the next hour. They didn't speak but it was a companionable silence. When she whispered that she was going to try and get a few hours' sleep, the warmth she'd brought into the room left with her.

Time dragged on. The clock on the wall ticked slowly.

The first hint of daylight seeped through the curtains.

Needing to stretch his legs, Massimo got to his feet and walked to his grandfather's dressing table. His mother had placed a dozen framed photos on it for him, his grandparents' wedding photo taking pride of place. Massimo picked it up and smiled sadly at the two beaming faces. How young they had been. How happy. And how in love. They'd met during his grandfather's deployment in the Second World War. His grandmother, who'd come from a wealthy English family, had worked for a secret government agency during that period. She'd kept those secrets for all her life. The only concrete facts Massimo knew were that they had met and fallen in love. His grandfather had left his home on the other side of the world permanently to marry her. Her parents, dismayed that she'd fallen for a man with skin they considered too dark, had disowned her. Massimo's grandparents had never allowed their subsequent poverty to get them down. They'd got on with life as best they could, raising a daughter, Sera, who was their pride and joy. When Sera married the Italian Gianni Briatore, they hadn't hesitated to follow her to Italy and make it their home.

He tried to imagine the challenges they'd faced. A mixed race couple in a time when mixed race marriages were frowned upon and in a time when most of the world was reeling from unimaginable horrors. Yet they had remained strong. Their love had endured. He didn't think it a coincidence that his grandfather was first diagnosed with cancer within a year of his grandmother's death.

His hand trembled as he placed the frame back on the dresser. His knuckles brushed the picture next to it, the one photo he'd spent two days blurring from his vision. This time, he picked it up.

It was his own wedding photo. He and Livia were in the centre, his parents to his left, his sister and grandfather to Livia's right.

If smiles could be converted into energy, Livia's could have powered a small country.

Massimo's own joy was there too on his beaming face. The camera didn't show that Livia's hand had been squeezing his bottom when the photo was taken.

Their wedding day had been the happiest of his life.

His grandfather coughed.

Abandoning the photo, Massimo hurried to his side and took his hand.

His grandfather's eyes were open. He coughed again. And then he smiled.

The love behind that smile could have fuelled the same country as Livia's and it filled Massimo's chest and spread through his veins.

He returned the smile.

He didn't notice the tear that had leaked from his eye until it rolled down his chin and landed on their joined hands.

The filmy eyes closed and his grandfather drifted back to sleep.

He never woke up again.

Three hours later, with the family he loved at his side, Jimmy Seibua took his last breath.

Livia switched the dishwasher on and dried her hands absently on the front of her black trousers, wishing there were something else she could do but there wasn't a single mark left to wipe down. She'd scrubbed the kitchen so hard it gleamed.

She felt heartsick to her core.

She'd sat with her brother during the full

Requiem mass for Jimmy. Gianluca had held her hand and kept her supplied with tissues. She was so proud of him and grateful for his support but she couldn't stop her heart from wishing it were Massimo's hand she'd been holding.

Stupid heart. One day it would catch up with her brain and let him go for good. All the resolutions she'd made had been destroyed before she'd had a chance to put them into practice.

But what else could she have done? Massimo's family had wanted her there while they'd nursed Jimmy in his final days. She'd wanted to be there too, with the old man who'd given her the most precious gift she could have received. A family.

The wake was being held in a marquee in the garden of Sera and Gianni's home. Caterers had been brought in for the refreshments, allowing family and friends to drink and reminisce his memory unhindered.

After an hour of it, Livia had needed to escape and slipped into the house to hide in the kitchen. Massimo's immediate family knew now they were getting divorced. He'd told them shortly after Jimmy's death. All had privately told her that their marriage was their own business but, divorce or not, she would always be family to them.

She wished that could be true and wished that when she said goodbye to them all later it wouldn't be for the last time.

She needed a clean break. There was no way she could move forward with her life if Massimo's family remained a central part of it. She would be permanently reminded of all she had lost.

She hoped they understood. She hoped they could forgive her.

'What are you doing?'

She turned her head to find Massimo at the kitchen door, his brow creased. His suit looked slightly baggy. Unsurprisingly, Massimo had lost weight. Livia doubted he'd eaten a full meal since they'd left the island.

She supposed he would go back to LA tonight. She was surprised he hadn't gone back after Jimmy's death and returned for the funeral. He'd stayed with his parents. She didn't think she was imagining the growing closeness between them. She could only hope it was a closeness that lasted.

'Cleaning up.'

'You didn't have to do that.'

She shrugged and stared at the floor. It hurt too much to look at him. 'I wanted to.'

Massimo closed the door and stood with his back to it. 'I want to thank you.'

'For what?'

'Everything you did for my grandfather and for all the support you've given my family.'

She raised her shoulders. It wasn't a shrug but he knew what she was trying to convey. That she didn't want or expect thanks. It was something she'd done because it was the right thing to do and because she couldn't not do it.

He wondered if she had any idea what a difference she'd made this last week.

Their last conversation before his grandfather had been taken ill…he'd hurt her so badly. She'd put her heart and her pride on the line for them to have a future together and he'd thrown it back at her and denounced the love they'd shared as anything worth fighting for.

And yet here she was, still there, still giving

the support he'd once taken for granted. Because he had taken it for granted. He'd become so damned frightened of his own feelings that he'd forgotten how good it had felt to go home and unload what was on his mind to her receptive ears and to lie in her arms and feel her massage the tension from his head and his shoulders. The errors he'd made... They hadn't been Livia's fault. They'd been his alone. But he'd punished her for them.

He'd pushed her away and shut her out one cold retreat at a time when he should have wrapped his arms around her and told her he loved her every single day.

After the funeral service, she'd joined the line of mourners waiting their turn to give their personal embrace to Massimo, his sister and their parents. She should have been by his side.

If she'd been at his side and he'd had her strength to lean on he would have found it easier to endure. He'd found everything easier to endure with Livia by his side. He'd forgotten that too.

'When are you going home?' she asked, breaking the silence.

'Tonight.'

'What's happened with the prototype?'

'Nothing. I've deferred the testing again until I get back.'

The raise of her shoulder seemed to indicate something different from her first raise but this was a shrug he couldn't interpret.

'Come back with me.' The words left his mouth before he could stop them.

Her eyes shot up to meet his. 'What?'

He rested the back of his head against the door as everything suddenly became clear. 'Come back with me. To Los Angeles.'

She just stared at him, lips parted but no sound coming out.

'Those things I said on the island. I didn't mean them…'

'They sounded convincing to me.'

'I love you.' And as he said the words aloud he felt a physical shift inside him.

'No!' Her voice ricocheted through the kitchen like a bullet.

'Livia—'

'I don't want to hear it.' She pressed her hands to her ears then finally met his eye. The pain reflecting back at him almost tore him in two. 'And I don't want to be the salve for your grief.'

'It's not about my grief.' How had he been so *blind*? 'I've been…'

'I don't want to hear another word of your lies.' Her shoulders rose in shudders and her throat moved before she turned away to take her bag from the counter. 'It's too late. I don't believe you. And even if I did, the answer would still be no. I could never trust my heart with you again.' She slung the strap of her bag over her shoulder and stood before him. When her eyes met his this time, they were devoid of emotion. 'I need to go.'

Something cold scratched deep in his throat.

He'd never fully recognised the love that had always reflected back at him until now that it was gone.

He moved to one side to let her pass.

She walked out of the kitchen without looking back.

When he could no longer hear her footsteps

and all that remained was the lightest linger of her fragrance, his knees finally gave way and he sank to the floor.

Head clasped in his hands, he breathed in deeply, calling himself every name under the sun until he could hold it back no longer and punched the nearest cabinet.

The crack it made echoed through the walls closing in around him.

He brought his hand to his face. Blood poured from his knuckles but he felt no pain.

The only pain came from the bleeding in his heart.

His grandfather's words at his party about having lived… Finally he understood them.

For the first time since he'd been a small child, Massimo wept.

He understood *everything*.

He understood that the blood in his veins never pumped as hard as it did when he was with Livia. She brought him to life. She had brought him back to his family. She had brought joy and love to his cold heart. She had lit the way and pulled him out of the darkness he hadn't realised he'd become lost in.

He understood, finally, that he could live in the warmth of her love or die in the cold of that darkness.

Livia hauled the shopping bags into the ground-floor apartment and closed the door with her bottom, craning her ears for the sound of the gaming console. Since she'd returned to her apartment after Jimmy's funeral two weeks ago, the sound of fast cars racing had become the background music of her life. She never complained about it. She needed the noise to drown the sound of her tortured thoughts.

Today, though, the apartment was quiet.

'Gianluca?' she called.

Her brother appeared as she was putting the bags on the side.

'Guess what?' he said, grinning and waving his phone in that goofy way of his.

'What?'

He looked as proud as a strutting peacock. 'Massimo's giving me a job.'

The name landed like a cold sharp shock against her face, just as it did every time Gianluca uttered it. She took a moment to compose herself. 'A job? Working for him? You're moving to America?'

His grin widened. 'You're not getting rid of me that easily. He's opening his European headquarters in Rome and has offered me a job on the security team.'

'He's opening headquarters *here*?'

Gianluca had the grace to look sheepish. 'He told me his plans the night of Jimmy's funeral after you'd gone but said not to say anything until everything was confirmed.'

So desperate had Livia been to get away from Massimo that she'd left the wake without her brother. Gianluca hadn't cared that she'd forgotten him. He'd had a great time getting drunk on bourbon with Massimo.

'You were told not to tell me?'

The sheepish expression morphed into the same confusion as she knew she must be showing. 'He didn't say not to tell you specifically. Just said it was best to keep it quiet until he'd bought the premises and knew for certain it would go ahead.' The confusion turned into beaming pride. 'And I kept my mouth shut exactly as he asked.'

'You certainly did. A job in security?' That was quite a step for an eighteen-year-old who'd never held down a job and had left school with only minimal qualifications. She had to practically crack her skin to get a smile to form. 'This is wonderful news. Congratulations. I didn't realise the two of you had kept in touch,' she added casually.

She should have guessed though. Since Massimo had brought in the team to help Gianluca escape the Secondigliano without reprisals, her brother had developed a serious case of hero worship.

Hearing him go on and on about how marvellous her estranged husband was... It was frustrating, to put it mildly. But she had the sense to reason with herself that if her brother was going to hero-worship anyone and use them as a base to model himself on, better it be Massimo than one of the men who had terrorised their lives.

'He's going to pay for me to take some courses too, so I can build on my qualifications. He said if I work hard, I could one day run his security for him.'

'This is wonderful,' she repeated. And it was. Truly. Livia had tried very hard not to be concerned that her brother hadn't been actively looking for work, telling herself he needed time to get used to this new life in a new city without the safety net of their family and his friends. She'd planned to give him a month to settle in before broaching the subject, when all along Massimo had already decided to give him a chance.

That was a big thing for him to do, she acknowledged. He knew full well what a handful Gianluca could be.

Handful or not, she'd been glad to have him around, and not only because it meant he was safe. His playful puppy-like ways were a welcome distraction from the painful ache in her frozen heart.

She dug into one of the shopping bags, pulled out the fresh tagliatelle she'd purchased and threw it at him.

He caught it easily.

'Put the water on and get this cooked. There's ricotta and spinach in the other bag. I'm going back to the shop to buy a bottle of prosecco. We need to celebrate!'

She hurried out of the apartment, Gianluca's protests that he didn't know how to cook pasta a distant ringing in her ears.

As soon as the door shut behind her, her smile dropped.

She walked down the street, her mind in a whirl.

Massimo was opening a headquarters here? In the city she lived in? The city he'd actively avoided throughout their marriage?

He'd once mooted the idea of opening a headquarters in London but that had been over a year ago, a throwaway musing of an idea. He hadn't mentioned it when they'd been in Fiji…

She firmly pushed the thought of Fiji from her mind. Every time a memory from it flashed through her, the nausea that seemed to have become a constant presence in her stomach swirled harder. It swirled now, strong enough to make her giddy.

As she passed a steakhouse, a customer opened its doors, unleashing the aromas being cooked within. Smells she would normally find tempting swirled through Livia's airways, increasing the nausea.

Suddenly fearing she really was going to be sick, she rested one hand against a wall, the other to her roiling stomach and forced as much air as she could into her lungs.

It seemed to take an age to pass.

When she finally felt capable of continuing, she looked up, but instead of her gaze fixing on the shop she was heading for, it landed on the neon-green cross on the other side of the street.

She didn't even realise she was staring at it until a small child walked into her. The mother, who was pushing a pram with a tiny baby in it, apologised but her words sounded like an echo in Livia's ears.

Thoughts of prosecco all but forgotten, she crossed the busy road and entered the pharmacy.

She'd stopped taking her pill when she'd left Massimo. They hadn't used protection when they were in Fiji. The thought hadn't even occurred to her, not even when she'd cuddled baby Elizabeth or when they'd had that angry conversation about babies.

Why had that been? She'd taken her pill religiously throughout their marriage. She'd wanted a baby with Massimo but it had been something they'd both agreed was for the future. And then their marriage had become so cold that it would have been cruel to bring a baby into it.

Two minutes later she walked out, a pregnancy test tucked in her bag.

Twenty minutes after that she was back in her apartment and in the bathroom, having given Gianluca the cash to go out and buy them food—he'd burnt the tagliatelle—and prosecco.

But he would have to drink the prosecco himself.

The test was unambiguous. She was pregnant.

Her head swimming, she did the only thing that made sense. She reached into her bag for her phone and called Massimo.

He answered on the third ring. 'Liv?'

Just hearing his voice made her heart clench and tears fill her eyes.

She squeezed them shut.

'Livia? Are you there? Is something wrong?'

She could hardly hear her own dull voice over the roar in her ears. 'I'm pregnant.'

CHAPTER FOURTEEN

THE SUDDEN PEAL of the doorbell only added to the pounding in Livia's head.

'If it's for me, I'm not in,' she shouted to her brother, who was playing on his games console in the living room.

Mercifully, Gianluca was a selfish teenager and had been oblivious to there being anything wrong with her when he'd returned with their takeaway. He'd also been oblivious when she'd eaten only half of her portion, using her lack of appetite as an opportunity to consume more food for himself, and oblivious to there being anything out of the ordinary when she'd announced immediately after eating that she was going to get an early night.

The bell rang again.

Grabbing her pillow, she pulled it over her head and burrowed deeper under the covers.

She would wallow for one night, she'd decided. Discovering she was pregnant was an exceptional circumstance that merited wallowing.

But…

For all the fear an unexpected pregnancy had brought there had also been the first flutterings of excitement.

Deciding that suffocating herself was probably bad for the baby, she removed the pillow and put it back under her head and stared at the ceiling.

She put a tentative hand up her nightshirt and pressed it against her belly. It didn't feel any different but a tiny life form was growing in there. A life created by her and Massimo.

Massimo…

She closed her eyes.

She couldn't decide if fate was being cruel or kind. When she'd finally found the strength to move forward with her life it played this most magical of tricks on her. She would never be free of him now.

She'd struggled to move on as it was. She'd kept a smile on her face, used iron willpower to stop herself biting her nails and gone through the motions of reclaiming her life but the wrench in her heart hadn't even started to heal yet.

She lived in hope rather than expectation.

She lived with an ache that left her always feeling cold. The sun could shine as hard as it wanted but she never felt it any more.

A knock on her bedroom door interrupted her wallowing.

She sat up, expecting Gianluca's face to appear and the request of money to be given.

But it wasn't her skinny brother who walked into her bedroom.

She blinked a number of times, certain she must be imagining the towering figure standing there, dressed in snug black jeans, a black T-shirt and a tan leather jacket. Her immediate impression was that he hadn't shaved since his grandfather's funeral.

She had to clear her throat to get any words out. 'What are you doing here?'

Massimo closed the door and gazed at the woman he loved sitting like a princess in her bed. He soaked in every detail of the face he'd missed so much.

'You didn't think I would take the news of you being pregnant and not come straight to you?'

Her brow creased in confusion. 'Do you have a time portal? I only told you two hours ago?'

'I would have been here sooner but I couldn't find my car keys and I'd already sent my driver home for the night. I walked.'

'You were already in Rome?'

'I never left.'

Now her whole face creased.

He grinned and removed his jacket, draping it over her dressing-table chair without taking his eyes from her. God, it felt so good seeing her. Knowing he was in the same city as Livia but unable to reach out to her had almost killed him. He took a step towards her. 'I've bought a house here.'

She shrank back as if afraid he was going to touch her. 'Since when?'

'The sale went through yesterday. I was going to wait a little longer for a few of the other pieces to fall into place before I came to you.'

The wariness in her eyes almost killed him too. 'Came to me for what?'

'To see what else it would take for you to believe that I do love you and that you can trust your heart with me.'

Since his epiphany at his grandfather's funeral, he'd done a lot of thinking.

Everything Livia had said about him was true. He did shut people out. Livia was the only person he'd ever let in but the moment he'd felt her get too close, the moment his heart had truly opened for her, he'd slammed it back shut and pushed her away.

He'd got so used to doing everything for himself, to relying only on himself that he'd convinced himself that it was the only way to be. He'd got so used to everything he touched turning into gold that when he'd made the first basic errors of his career he'd automatically blamed Livia for them, forgetting that he was only human.

She'd brought such joy into his life and, fool

that he was, he'd turned his back on that joy and turned his back on her.

He'd pushed his parents away too. He'd been a condescending, arrogant bastard about the choices they'd made. They'd chosen family over money and he'd been too blind to appreciate the sacrifices they'd made so he could have that security. He'd taken their love for granted. He'd never had to walk his sister to school or cook her meals as Livia had done for Gianluca. He'd never slept with a weapon under his pillow out of fear. The threadbare clothes he'd been so ashamed to wear had always been lovingly repaired, the holes in his shoes fixed until the shoes could be replaced. He'd been so focused on creating his own future that he'd never taken the time to appreciate all the things he'd had right there. Love. Security. An abundance of affection. All the things that when added together made life worth living.

He'd been blind about everything.

But Livia had seen everything clearly.

He didn't blame her for dismissing his half-formed declaration of love.

Along with all his thinking he'd done a lot of doing.

The path to bringing her back into his life had been clear. He'd needed to rebuild her trust with actions rather than words.

Her shoulders rose before she brought her knees up and wrapped her arms around them. 'Not this again,' she whispered. 'I told you, it's too late. I've moved on.'

'Nature doesn't think so or you wouldn't be pregnant.'

'Nature is a joke.'

'A wonderful joke.'

She rested her chin on her knees. 'You're happy?'

'That we're having a baby together? Liv, there is only one thing that could make me happier than I feel at this moment but I will get to that shortly. Why didn't you tell me you'd come off the pill?'

Colour flamed her cheeks. 'I didn't think.'

'And I didn't think to ask if you were still on it.' He pulled his T-shirt over his head.

'What are you doing?' she asked, alarm in her voice but something different in her eyes.

'Showing you something.' Dropping the T-shirt on the floor, he kicked his boots off and climbed onto the bed. Then he leaned forward to take her rigid hand and placed it on his left bicep. Eyes holding hers, he said, 'The spearheads on this tattoo… One of the meanings for it is willpower. I had it done to remind myself to remain strong. I needed that reminder when you left me otherwise I would have chased after you and begged you to come back to me.'

He moved her hand so it rested on his chest above his beating heart. 'I married you because the madness of my attraction to you compelled me to. I knew my feelings for you ran deep and I assumed what I felt for you was love but I didn't know it could grow deeper. I didn't know my feelings for you would take root in my soul and that you would become my reason for breathing. You challenged me on so many levels I didn't know where I ended and you began. When you left me I felt as if I'd been freed from madness itself. I threw myself back into my work a liberated man and I would have worked myself into an early grave rather than stop for a minute and open myself to the pain beating right here in this cold, shrivelled heart that losing you caused.'

He reached for her hair with his free hand and ran his fingers down the silky locks he loved so much. 'I'm sorry for pushing you away. I'm sorry for shutting you out. I'm sorry for throwing your love back at you and demeaning everything we meant to each other. I'm sorry for every minute of hurt I caused you.'

She opened her mouth but he put a finger to her lips.

'I'm sorry for doing nothing when I knew how miserable you were in LA.'

'Don't,' she whispered, turning her cheek. 'My loneliness was my fault too. I should have gone out and had English lessons and taken art classes or something.'

'Art classes?'

She shrugged. 'Something that got me out of the house. Something that stopped me being dependent on you for my happiness.'

That reminded him of something he'd meant to ask her on the island. 'Have you had English lessons since we separated?'

'I started an online course. I didn't get very far. My head wasn't in the right place for new information to sink into it.'

He rubbed his thumb along her cheekbone, his heart swelling. 'There was a lot I could have done to make your life easier and if you come back to me, I swear things will be different. I'm moving back to Italy.'

Her eyes found his again. There was a glimmer of something in them that gave him hope.

'Everything you said before we left the island was right, including what you said about my relationship with my family,' he said quietly. 'How can I build a proper relationship with them if I'm living on the other side of the ocean?'

'Is that why you're opening a base here in Rome?'

He nodded and slid his hands down her cheeks to cup her face. 'Partly. But mostly for you. Your life is here and my life is with you... if you'll let me back in it. That's all I want. To be with you. It took losing you for me to see how much I need you.'

A tear spilled out and rolled down her cheek

and over his hand. 'You said that about our marriage. That you hadn't realised how un-suited you were to marriage until you married me.'

'I said a lot of things. I believed a lot of things.'

'So why should I believe you now?' Livia wanted to believe him more desperately than she had ever wanted to believe anything but she was frightened. Her heart had been wrung too many times to bloom properly any more.

'Because now my head is clear. I want to make our marriage work more than I have ever wanted anything and I'm willing to do whatever it takes for it. You're my priority, now and for ever…you and our baby.' He could hardly believe he was going to be a father. 'I was waiting for confirmation of the sale of my house in LA before I came to you…' He gave a rueful smile. 'Your news about the pregnancy brought me to you a few days earlier than I anticipated. I wanted to be able to look you in the eye and give you categorical proof that you're more important to me than anything else. The house I've bought here in Rome is in your name.' Another rueful smile. 'I'm hoping you will let me share it with you. If not, it's yours to keep. I'll still need a base in LA but I'm hoping you'll come with me and choose a house for us to share there. A house you're comfortable in, in a neighbourhood you can feel at home in. There's a lot that I'm hoping for but whatever happens from this point forward is up to you.'

'And what if I say no?'

He closed his eyes and inhaled deeply through his nose. 'Then I will have only myself to blame and I will have to be content with having a child with you even if I can't be your husband. All I would ask is that you allow me to be a proper father to it.'

Livia blinked back the fresh tears blurring her vision so she could look at him properly.

Ringing from the soulful caramel eyes was nothing but sincerity.

Her heart thumped and expanded.

'Let me get a few things straight,' she said slowly. 'In the last two weeks you've bought me a house, bought new business premises here in Rome, offered my delinquent brother a job and put your house up for sale in LA. Have I missed anything?'

'I think that's everything.'

'And you've done all this for me?'

He shifted forward and pressed the tip of his nose to hers. 'You're my life, Livia. Everything I have is yours.'

Her heart expanding a little more, she nudged her face a little closer to place the softest of kisses to his lips. 'I need you to promise me something.'

'Anything.'

Her hands crept onto his shoulders. 'Don't ever push me away again.'

'Never.' Now he placed the softest of kisses to her lips. 'Does this mean...?'

She hooked her hands around his neck. The blooming in her heart was growing with every breath she took. Staring deep into his eyes, she smiled. 'It means yes. To everything.'

The eyes staring back at her were searching. 'Do you think you can ever love me again?'

She kissed him once more and kept her mouth there, breathing him in, filling her lungs and her senses with the taste and scent she'd believed she would never enjoy again. She moved her lips away long enough to say, 'Massimo, you are etched in my heart. I've loved you since the day I met you and I will love you until the day I die.'

'You're etched on my heart too. And my soul. There is only you.'

And with those words her blooming heart swelled and reached out to join with his for ever.

A long while later, naked and replete in each other's arms, Massimo suddenly pulled himself out of the light sleep he'd fallen into.

With everything that had happened that evening, the full, wonderful magnitude of their situation finally hit him. 'We're having a baby.'

Livia giggled softly and kissed his chest. 'Yes, we are!'

'Have I told you recently how much I love you?'

'Not recently enough.'

He told her. And then he showed her.

EPILOGUE

LIVIA STOOD AT the front of the chalet's veranda, her hands on the wooden balustrade, and watched in awe at the rain lashing down. From her vantage point, she could see the main part of Seibua Island and all the surrounding ocean.

In the distance, she spotted one of the staff running through the rain in exaggerated leaps and grinned. If baby Sera weren't sleeping in her crib, Livia would be out there running a dance through it too. Massimo thought her a little bit mad for loving the rainy season so much but for her it was perfect. It unleashed Seibua Island's scents so that even the dullest of them filled the air with their potency and made the landscape a glimmering sheen of verdant brilliance. The rainbows that came when the sun blazed through the rain were the most glorious sight. She hoped one appeared soon.

The buzzing of her phone distracted her from her rainbow watch and she pulled it out of her shorts pocket, rolling her eyes at yet another of her brother's joke messages. She quickly fired a message back telling him he should be working and got an indignant reply that it was early morning in Rome and even the birds weren't awake yet. Smiling widely, she put her phone back in her pocket and resumed her position on the veranda.

While she scanned in all directions, she saw her mother-in-law poke her head out of her chalet door and laughed when she immediately whipped it back in.

In truth, it wasn't only Massimo who thought her a little mad for her love of the rain. His entire family thought the same. None of them understood how magical she found it, how without it there would be no rainbows and none of the glorious colour that now filled her life.

She remembered reading something once,

how without the dark we wouldn't see the stars. That was how she felt about the rain.

She laughed again when she saw Jimmy make his escape from the lodge to go dancing in it as he'd watched her do numerous times. He saw her looking and waved wildly.

She waved back, waving harder when Massimo, who'd been caught in the lodge when the downpour started, came out to join their three-year-old son, his bemusement obvious even from the distance that separated them.

Her heart swelled to see him scoop their son into his arms and swing him around. She didn't need to be close to hear Jimmy's squeal of laughter. It was a sound locked in her memory bank.

And then her heart swelled enough to burst when, right above their dancing heads, the clouds parted and the multicoloured arc appeared in all its glory.

It appeared to be shining just for them.

* * * * *

LET'S TALK

For exclusive extracts, competitions
and special offers, find us online:

- facebook.com/millsandboon
- @millsandboonuk
- @millsandboon

Or get in touch on 0844 844 1351*

For all the latest titles coming soon,
visit millsandboon.co.uk/nextmonth

*Calls cost 7p per minute plus your phone company's price per
minute access charge

Want even more
ROMANCE?

Join our bookclub today!

'Mills & Boon books, the perfect way to escape for an hour or so.'

Miss W. Dyer

'Excellent service, promptly delivered and very good subscription choices.'

Miss A. Pearson

'You get fantastic special offers and the chance to get books before they hit the shops'

Mrs V. Hall

Visit millsandbook.co.uk/Bookclub and save on brand new books.

MILLS & BOON